EVERY GOOD WORK

A CHRISTIAN SUSPENSE NOVEL

URCELIA TEIXEIRA

EVERY GOOD WORK

AN ADAM CROSS CHRISTIAN SUSPENSE

URCELIA TEIXEIRA

Copyrighted material
Ebook © ISBN: 978-1-928537-73-1
Paperback © ISBN: 978-1-928537-74-8
Independently Published by Urcelia Teixeira
First edition
Urcelia Teixeira
Wiltshire, UK

www.urcelia.com
books@urcelia.com

To Mom
You were the first to teach me about God.
You were the first to show me His good works in your
own life,
and you were the first to allow Him to work in mine.
You taught me perseverance in faith,
what it means to trust Him.
You showed me your unshaken faith,
prayed for and encouraged me without ceasing.
Thank you
x

INSPIRED BY

"For it is by grace you have been saved, through faith—
and this not from yourselves, it is the gift of God—not
by works, so that no one can boast."
Ephesians 2:8-9
(NIV)

CHAPTER ONE

I t only took an instant to realize that he was already dead when Patrick Phillips dropped to his knees next to the lifeless body of his client.

Dr. Bill Sutton's blank eyes stared into the space next to him, as though focused on something unseen. Fresh blood drenched the plush cream rug beneath his shoulders in his home office.

As if he wasn't convinced Bill was dead, Patrick leaned in to better inspect his face only to discover the horrific gash across his neck. He had never seen a dead body before, and it took every bit of inner strength to hold down the caviar he had enjoyed with Bill just a short while ago.

His heart pounded hard against his chest as his body now trembled with shock. Next to his knees, the pool of blood threatened to soak the designer suit he had specially bought for that evening's charity dinner. Jumping to his feet he stepped away from the body and stood anxiously staring at it with both hands clasped on top of his head.

In the background, he heard the dinner guests' chatter coming from the reception room at the end of the corridor. Suddenly aware that anyone could walk in on him at any moment, he panicked and rushed to close the door he had inadvertently left ajar. He needed time to think, time to make sure they wouldn't implicate him.

If caught alone in the room with the great Dr. Bill Sutton lying dead on the floor, it would take a lot more than his word to convince authorities he wasn't to blame. Why he felt such immense guilt over his death, he didn't know. Perhaps because deep down inside he had wished Bill dead a million times. To the world out there Dr. Bill Sutton was a saint, a savior of lives. But to him, Bill was the proverbial nightmare client no one wanted. The only reason he'd tolerated his condescending ways with him was because he was best friends with his son, William. And Bill had made it abundantly clear that his loyalty to his only son was the single reason he had agreed to let Patrick manage the company's financial portfolio. So they were each doing it for William. On that, they could agree. Everything else, not so much.

It was also no secret that Bill hadn't been pleased with his recent trading strategies. Patrick had lost him millions in a swing trade. He'd heard the rumors—Bill had been shopping around for a new portfolio manager. Without the Gencorp account, Patrick's company wouldn't even exist. Everyone knew that, and with Bill out of the way, William, his only son, and heir to Bill's entire fortune, would make void that threat.

That was motive.

He'd need solid evidence, an alibi.

And he had neither.

Patrick nervously circled Bill's dead body, careful not to step into the blood or leave any trace behind. With his palms now together over his nose and mouth, he took a deep breath to relax his shoulders and snapped the vertebrae in his neck back into place. He was used to thinking on his feet, deciding under pressure. Risk management was the very marrow in his bones.

With his eyes fixed on the dead body on the floor, his mind hurriedly worked through the dilemma. He was last seen flirting with Bill's attractive assistant before he made small talk with a few prospective clients. As far as anyone should be aware, he was still out there canvassing the room for new clients. Bill had joined a few of the other guests in the wine cellar. At least that's what Patrick had assumed when Bill had excused himself and walked off in that direction.

Patrick's mind worked through the events of the evening. If only he hadn't come looking for Bill. If only he hadn't felt so insecure over losing the Gencorp account and tried so hard to win back Bill's favor.

There was no doubt in his mind. He'd definitely be on the police's main suspect list. A list that wasn't that long. Bill didn't have enemies—he was far too good-natured for that.

The reflection triggered him to realize that his fingerprints were on the doorknob. He leaped across the room and, using his pocket square, wiped the handles on either side of the door. Pausing at the door, he readied himself to quietly sneak out but quickly let go of the notion when he heard footsteps approaching. Frazzled by the unexpected threat, his eyes searched for a place to hide as the footsteps grew closer. Moments before the doorknob turned to open the door, Patrick hid in a dark shadowy space between a floor-to-ceiling bookcase and a wall in one corner of the room. Unable to see the door, he stood there, shoulders squashed between the wall and the bookcase, his back stiff and his body on high alert. All he saw was Bill's unresponsive eyes staring directly at him. It made his stomach tense up; it was downright creepy, so he looked down at his feet instead. The door creaked open, then gently closed again. As he waited, barely breathing, he spotted a small oxblood leather notebook next to his feet on the floor. Intrigued, his eyes remained fixed on it while he listened for movement in the room. His instincts told him it had to have been the killer who had returned, and he guessed the book had something to do with it since Bill's eyes had fixed on it just before he died. If it were any of the guests, they'd have screamed by now.

He stood still, barely breathing as he listened. But the room was dead silent. It baffled him. What was he waiting for?

When, after a few moments, there was still no sign of anyone in the room, he slowly leaned forward and peered around the bookcase into the room. There was no one to be seen—at least not from his angle.

Perhaps the killer had left. Remaining cautious and alert, he bent to pick up the notebook. A shuffle to his right let him know he wasn't alone after all. It took a mere split second to be discovered by a man wearing a dark dinner suit and a black hooded mask with matching gloves.

Without another second to spare—for fear of being trapped in the corner—Patrick charged towards the door. But the masked figure was too quick, the silver blade of his knife glistening under the soft light of the overhead chandelier.

As quick as lightning, the killer's gloved hand thrust the knife forward and slashed across Patrick's arm. The sharp edge sliced through the sleeve of his suit and very nearly penetrated all the layers of his clothing. The motion had Patrick step back several paces, in the process nearly tripping over Bill's body.

"Who are you? What do you want?" Patrick yelled out.

The answer to one of his questions was obvious when, from behind the narrow slits in his hooded mask, the killer's beady eyes fixed on the leather notebook that was still clasped in Patrick's hand. With only Bill's body on the floor between them, there was little else to protect Patrick from ending up dead on the floor next to Bill.

"What's so important about this book that you'd kill a man over it, huh? Who are you?" Patrick asked again, hoping his questions would buy him some time until someone heard and came to his rescue.

The killer didn't answer. He'd seen through Patrick's futile attempt to escape his wrath. Instead, a silent, slow dance of sorts ensued between them as they circled around Bill's body, the knife in the killer's outstretched hand hovering, threatening. Neither of them made the first move. Neither of them spoke.

As they turned once more, and Patrick faced the French doors that opened out onto a small veranda that overlooked the bay, he cast a swift glance at the light-weight curtain that stirred ever so slightly in the evening breeze. He couldn't be certain the doors were open, but if not, he'd break his way through the glass. If he could somehow be quick enough, he could escape across the lawn and disappear between the boats in the marina. It was his only option. Fleeing through the internal door and the house would give the killer the perfect opportunity to get away, leaving him the one who'd end up looking like the murderer fleeing the scene.

Preparing for his escape, he placed the notebook in the inside breast pocket of his jacket, his face arrogantly mocking the killer.

The killer remained silent.

"You know you won't get away with this. There are cameras all over this place. Your days are numbered, buddy," Patrick bluffed, attempting to distract the killer.

It worked.

Patrick watched as his beady eyes darted to the corners of the study. Using it to his advantage, Patrick gently manipulated their circular dance until he had his back facing the terrace doors.

"You're missing the one above the entrance door behind you," he deceived again.

When the killer turned to look over his shoulder, Patrick swung around and bolted for the French doors, pushing a chair down behind him as he passed it. His mind was laser sharp and focused on the slight parting in the middle of the two doors. With no effort, his lean frame and agility had him slip through the opening with ease.

Adrenaline pulsed through his veins as he took two long strides before he hoisted himself over the low wood railing to land feet first into the shrubs below. He lost his footing and rolled onto the expansive lawns but, thanks to his athletic prowess, was back on his feet and running in no time. Behind him, the killer's feet hit the deck. Patrick didn't turn to look for fear of losing his focus. He ran. As fast as his feet would carry him. Down the slight hill, towards the glistening lights in the small marina. Mere steps behind him, he heard the killer's strained breathing under his face covering.

He pushed his body harder, keeping his eyes on the marina some eighty yards or so away. It took several more strides, but he had gained enough distance between them. When he reached the bottom of the hill where the grass met with the white concrete walkway that led another thirty yards down into the marina, his eyes skimmed over the moored boats. There were at least fifty, ranging from large luxury yachts and catamarans to smaller sailboats. Spaced evenly along the now wooden walkway, the warm glow of overhead lamps illuminated every step he took. He'd need to get out of the light and hide—quickly.

Up ahead, positioned in the shadows between two lamps, he spotted a jetty leading off into the darkness between the boats. When he reached it, he quickly turned onto the floating jetty that ran between the two rows of large yachts. Hiding in one of the vessels wouldn't do. With only five of them on either side, it would be dead easy for the killer to find him. If he had any chance of escaping, he'd have to get into the water. Short on options, and short on time, he didn't hesitate.

When he reached the smaller landing stage between two enormous black yachts, he quickly stepped onto it, nearly losing his balance as the water moved beneath it.

Obscured by the large vessels, he retrieved the pocket-sized book from his jacket and secured it between his teeth.

Behind him, he heard the main jetty grind against the guide ropes as the killer's weight slowly moved over it toward him.

CHAPTER TWO

The water was colder than he had expected and he drew in a sharp breath, nearly causing the notebook to slip out from between his teeth.

Holding onto the side of the yacht, he gently lowered himself into the water, careful not to be heard.

Gentle waves lapped against his torso as the water hit the side of the vessel—it was close to high tide. As he quietly glided between the boats, the water's motion pushed the yachts closer together, threatening to crush him between the buoys. He swam faster, causing more noise than he wanted to, but it was a risk he had to take. And it paid off. He made it just in time before the yachts closed the gap behind him.

Although he was an excellent swimmer, swimming with stealth while biting down on a book between his teeth made it much harder. For the briefest of moments, he wondered if it was worth holding onto, worth dying for. But just as quickly, a deep sense of loyalty to William compelled him to continue. He owed him that much. Whatever information that book contained was important enough for his father to die. And he deserved to know why.

A few more strokes delivered him to the furthest end of the next row of moored boats. Desperate to draw in a few proper breaths, and eager to assess the killer's position, he clung to a rope on the back of one of the smaller sailboats. With one arm curled around the rope, he took the book from his mouth and, holding it above his head, drew in a few deep breaths. From his shadowy vantage point, the killer's dark frame came into view on top of a boat opposite him. Seconds later, the shrill sound of police sirens coming from the direction of Bill's house rang through the quiet night air. It had the killer's body suddenly upright and at attention. Barking dogs and male voices shouting commands at each other soon followed, warning the killer that a search was already underway. The killer didn't need any more convincing, and he took off along the jetty and across the marina faster than a bolt of lightning. Relieved as Patrick was, he knew that he too was at risk of being found by the police. He considered sneaking back into the house and melting among the guests, but that wasn't an option. For one thing, he was drenched, and for another, he was horrible at lying.

With the book back between his teeth, he pulled his body up and into the boat. Taking a moment, he glanced around. It wasn't as big as most of the others—about thirty or forty feet, and while it had a sail, it relieved him to see it was also motorized. He knew his way around a sailboat. A skill his late father had taught him from a young age. Growing up in New York, escaping to the Hamptons for a weekend was a regular occurrence in his family, and sailing took up most of their time on these breaks.

Keeping his attention on the police search, he slipped his jacket off and wrung it out by twisting it around one of the nearby railing posts. The spring air nipped at his skin beneath his wet shirt, and although still damp, he slipped his now creased jacket back on.

With the notebook safely back inside his breast pocket, he made his way to the helm, keeping his eyes on the embankment for any signs of approaching police.

When his hands found the ignition and the dangling keys in it, he let out a suppressed giggle. That was so typical of the people who lived out there. So trusting of the neighborhood that they'd leave the keys in their boats. Yet a man got murdered right under their noses. The memory sent a fresh shiver down his spine. Propelled by the horrific event and the urgent need to get away, his feet moved swiftly across the deck to untie the yacht from its mooring before he dashed back to take up position behind the wheel.

The engine purred into motion as he turned the key. It made his heart skip several beats when he realized what he was doing. He had never stolen a single thing in his entire life. Not even a piece of candy from his mother's secret jar that only came out on Super Bowl Sunday. His mother would have had a fit had she been there.

As if his mother and the owner of the boat stood beside him, he spoke a quick apology into the cool night air and gave his index finger permission to hit the button with which to raise the anchor. Still riddled by guilt as he gently pulled the yacht out of its bay, he reasoned that he hardly had a choice in the matter at hand. He'd be walking straight into a police investigation if he went back to the house—with whatever deadly information the leather journal contained.

They would now have motive and evidence that he was at the scene of the crime.

Reflecting on the fresh implication he'd unknowingly brought upon himself, he cursed beneath his breath. Of all the stupid things he'd done, this one took the cake. He wondered how a man like Bill could've gotten himself so viciously killed. Bill wasn't the type to be involved with anything even remotely dishonest or illegal. Who would have had reason to kill a man as acclaimed for his good deeds as Bill? The man was practically a saint. It had to have been a mistake. A fatal one at that.

As he pointed the sailboat's nose toward the open waters, he looked back over his shoulder toward the house. Red and blue lights lit up the night sky at the front of the house, and he could just about make out a few police officers making their way down toward the marina. He turned the boat's lights off and nudged it forward, impressed with how silently it glided through the calm water.

When he was a fair way out of the marina and the house's sightline, he turned the lights back on and settled into cruising speed. He had evaded the killer successfully, and the police, but he didn't have the slightest idea where to go next. He could get off at one of the other marinas further along the coast, then find his way back to his apartment in Manhattan—say he left the party early. If he dropped the anchor just enough for the boat to not float away too far, they'd simply think the boat got loose and drifted down the coast. But it was close to midnight already and, apart from calling a taxi —which would then prove his whereabouts—he had no other means of transportation to get himself back home. Concluding his best option was to wait it out on the boat until the very early hours of the morning and then catch the train into the city, he pushed the throttle forward and continued further away from the shoreline.

Even though it was late spring, the night was chilly but beautiful. The water was calm, something rather unusual for that time of year. Almost too calm, he thought. He glanced up at the stars and filled his lungs with the fresh evening air. He loved sailing, albeit not under these circumstances. It was the one time he felt his father's presence the most. A dry lump formed in his throat as he recalled their last sailing trip together—a month before he collapsed in the middle of their lounge during a football game. It felt as if it was just yesterday.

He cleared his throat and wiped away the lonely tear that had lodged between his lower lashes. This was the first time he'd set sail since the day his father died, and he'd never needed his father's wisdom more.

PATRICK DROPPED ANCHOR ABOUT TWO NAUTICAL MILES off the coast. It was far out, he knew, but he needed to make sure no one would spot him from the shore. He was tired, starving, and with his suit still wet, frozen to the bone. With the boat firmly secured in position for the night, he slipped below deck in search of warm clothes and something to eat.

The yacht was modern, spacious, and immaculate. Decorated in crisp white with navy and red accents to match the color of the vessel's exterior, it was pure luxury. Patrick grinned from ear to ear.

"That's what I'm talking about," he gloated out loud.

Caught up in the moment, he flopped down onto one of the white cotton sofas and stretched his arms out over the backrest, extending his legs out and crossing them at the ankles. But his moment of glee was short-lived when his damp suit pinched in all the wrong places and forced him back onto his feet.

There were two cabins in the stern at either end of the boat. He picked the larger of the two and went straight for the closet, relieved when he found several pieces of men's clothing.

"Well, at least you have good taste, Mr. Whoever-you-are," he said.

Satisfied with a pair of chinos, a designer white sweater, and a pair of tan leather deck shoes, he flung it all on top of the bed and grabbed a towel from the nearby bathroom. A few minutes later he was dry, warm, and had his now ruined suit hanging on a hanger to dry. Perhaps Fabricio's talented hands could work his tailoring magic and salvage it, he thought. The extravagant suit was the most expensive piece of clothing he had ever bought, all in the hope of signing a few new clients—and keeping up appearances in a world where he didn't really belong.

One more floor below deck brought him to the snug kitchen that resembled the one he had in his apartment. He grabbed two cans of soda from the fridge before finding a bag of potato chips and a box of already opened salt and pepper crackers he hoped weren't stale in one cupboard.

Upstairs and back on the white sofa, after downing

half the can of soda and several handfuls of chips, he wiped his palms on his pants and pulled the leather notebook from his pants' pocket where he had placed it after he had changed his clothes.

"Let's see what all the fuss is about, shall we?" he said out loud to himself.

Patrick ran the pages through his thumb, settling on a random page. There was nothing but lines and lines of numbers on every page. Numbers that weren't arranged in any particular order, or at first glance, that meant anything he could recognize.

"That's it, a bunch of stupid numbers. Really, Bill? This is what you got yourself killed over?" he said, as if Bill was in the boat with him.

He flung the notebook on top of the glossy white coffee table in front of him and stuffed a few more fists full of chips into his mouth.

While his mind worked ceaselessly through the night's events, and his body eagerly succumbed to the potato chips and soda, the soothing sound of the water that lapped against the hull soon had him drift off into a blissful sleep.

CHAPTER THREE

It was well into the night and Patrick had already been sleeping for several hours when a loud noise jolted him awake. He had fallen asleep on the sofa earlier that night and now sat up to find the yacht violently rocking from side to side so violently that it almost flung him off the sofa altogether.

Another loud noise above his head had him to his feet in an instant, but he battled to stay upright. Holding on to the furniture, he stumbled his way along the lower deck toward the exit that led up to the main deck, bending at the waist to look through the portholes along the way. It was pitch black outside, but he could hear the drumming sounds of rain as it pelted down onto the yacht all around him. The wind whistled noisily above his head while the boat's rigging clanked wildly against the mast.

Halfway up the steps toward the deck, he reached out to open the hatch. It took immense effort and he nearly lost his balance and fell on his back. Struggling against the violent swaying of the yacht, he gave it one hard push. As the hatch lifted away from the boat's frame, a strong wind nearly swept it, and him, away. Sheets of rain and an untimely wave that washed over the boat slammed into his face. It took the full weight of his body to close the hatch and secure it back into position. Unsteady on his feet, his body drenched, he clung onto the steps to contemplate the dire situation he now found himself in.

He had only once sailed in stormy conditions, and it had been once too many. But nothing like this one.

With his one arm curled around the arm rail, his feet apart to anchor himself to the swaying floor, he turned to see the readings on the navigational instruments to his right. At first, he thought his eyes were deceiving him, or that the instruments might be faulty, but when he moved closer and stood facing it, he quickly realized the tight feeling in his chest was for good reason. He jotted down the readings as best he could, considering his unstable footing. Wind speed, forty-five knots, water depth, changing between eighty-four and one hundred meters—the maximum depth the instrument measured. The next digit confirmed what he had already correctly estimated. Wave size, four to six meters.

Panic flooded his already tense body. The numbers

didn't lie. He'd got caught in a storm that measured nothing short of at least a medium tropical storm. He reached out to the dials on the VHF radio on the wall and began turning one clockwise to search for a transmission, cursing himself for forgetting one of the cardinal rules of safety when stepping onboard a vessel. It would have taken no effort at all to listen to the weather forecast the moment he set sail.

With shaky fingers, he turned the dial in search of any weather information or warnings.

There was no signal.

Another loud bang scared him witless as the wind slammed an unfamiliar object against the porthole directly to his left. The noise surprised him and the sudden movement threw him off balance. He fell to the ground, lost control over his body as it slid along the wet floor, and crashed into the side of one sofa. When he finally regained control over his limbs, he pulled himself back to the indoor bridge and reached for the transceiver.

"Mayday, mayday! Can anyone hear me?"

There was no answer.

He called out again. Still nothing.

Turning the dial in both directions, he continued to search for a channel, all the while clinging on to whatever he could to keep himself upright.

But his calls for help remained unanswered.

It didn't take him long to realize that the effects of

the weather were too great and that he was either out of range, or the antenna had gotten damaged. The possibility of it being the latter had his heart skip several beats.

But Patrick Phillips was by nature a fighter. Or perhaps it was his skill to assess risk and quickly plan solutions to problems. He wasn't sure, but he refused to give up.

He placed the transceiver back on its cradle. As he glanced outside the nearby porthole, a thunderous bolt of lightning flashed across the sky and lit up the mass of water around him. It took his breath away, confirming what the instruments had already told him. The momentary glimpse of what he was up against sent a fresh ripple down his spine. Overwhelmed with fear, his emotions rampant, he could soon no longer control his now rapid breathing. A multitude of fateful thoughts flooded his mind all at once, and he nearly allowed his legs to give way beneath his body.

But he fought the urge to collapse and refused to accept the impending watery death his mind was so eager to have him believe would be his fate.

He steadied himself, drew in several deep breaths, and took a stance at the cockpit.

"Stay calm, Patrick. Just keep it together, man," he told himself.

He snatched the map from the cubby above his head,

relieved that he'd at least remembered to mark his location when he had dropped anchor.

At the time he was two nautical miles off the coast, but even with his sails down, it would have been impossible for the boat to have held its position—not with an ocean depth beyond one hundred meters. His anchor cable simply didn't allow for that much depth. And with the swell so big, the currents had undoubtedly dragged him out to sea. He could be anywhere by now.

Worst is, no one knew he had stolen a yacht and set out to sea.

Over the next few minutes, Patrick studied the gauges and several locations on his map, but it was impossible to know his precise location without a stable reading from the instruments. Instead, he calculated a radius and noted it down. If he could somehow keep his position somewhat steady, he might have a chance at weathering the storm—and staying alive.

A plan took shape in his mind. One that presented itself as suicidal. But it was the only one he could come up with.

In a last attempt, he snatched the radio receiver off its cradle and tried calling for help again. But the line was still dead. Resolving he'd now have to execute Plan B, he searched for the emergency sat phone. If he could get up to the bridge, he could send up a distress signal and might also have a better chance at getting a satellite connection. Once on deck, he'd also release the anchor's brake to allow the chain's maximum length in the hope it would grab hold of something on the ocean floor.

Reaching into the cubby overhead, he snatched the waterproof pouch that contained the emergency pack he was after. It only took a few seconds for Patrick to slip the lifejacket over his head and secure it to his body. Next, he extended a bright orange safety lanyard and hurriedly slipped it around his waist at one end, holding onto the steel carabiner that was attached to the other end. The risk of him washing overboard was enormous, but he had no choice. If he were to have any chance of surviving this storm, he'd have to grab every opportunity at his disposal.

In the back of his mind, a niggling voice told him he would never make it out alive, and haunted by the thought of drowning and being plunged into a watery death, he turned around and took in the surrounding space—as if bidding it farewell. On the floor, several feet away, he spotted the notebook that had landed him in this predicament. He scoffed, insanely thinking it must derive pleasure from his torture.

"Not today, buddy. If I go down, you go down," he said as if it were alive.

Propelled by an irrational sense of victory over an enemy that carried no sane threat, he made his way over to the notebook and snatched it up before it could slide away. At first, he thought to keep it in his pants' pocket, but when an image of Bill's lifeless eyes flashed in his mind's eye, he suddenly felt the urge to protect it. If by some miracle he made it back to dry land, he would do whatever it took to find the killer—and most likely need it to prove he had nothing to do with Bill's murder.

Back at the cockpit, he sealed the notebook inside the waterproof pouch that had carried the emergency safety gear. With the flare gun secured in his waistband, he tossed the remaining contents to one side.

He then put on a bright yellow weather coat to which he clipped the sat phone on the provided safety hook below the lapel before doing the same with the sealed bag, tucking it inside his jacket. As he pushed toward the hatch, nerves settling into a tight knot inside his stomach, he drew in a deep breath and exhaled quickly—as if he was blowing out the candles on a birthday cake.

This time, aided by the strong winds, the hatch lifted away with ease and Patrick fought hard to secure the latch back in place behind him. Rain hit his face and eyes with force, and the strong winds threatened to sweep him off his feet more times than he cared to count. Securing the tether to the yacht's safety hooks, he dragged his body along the deck and eventually into the cockpit, sliding the tether between each safety support hook.

When several bolts of lightning lit up the ocean around him, he saw gigantic waves that hugged the vessel as far as his eyes could see. Strong winds which seemed to come from every direction tossed the boat from side to side. So great was the vessel's tilt between the waves that the top of the mast dipped into the crests. The sight left him near paralyzed with fear and he knew there was no way he would make it to the bow to release the anchor brake by hand.

Up on the bridge, his hands searched for the switch on the overhead spotlight as he shone the light out across the ocean to confirm what he had already seen. But there was no mistaking it. A massive storm that might very well take his life engulfed him.

"Mayday, mayday! This is Patrick Phillips. Can anyone hear me?" he called over the satellite phone.

Barely audible over the howling winds and rushing ocean noise, the line screeched.

He tried again, and again, but got no answer.

As he reached for the flare gun and shot off a single distress signal, a wave splashed over the top of the bridge and dumped an enormous amount of water onto the deck. He kept calling for help, moving through the channels, announcing his estimated location.

His hands ached where he had been gripping the wheel that had taken on a life of its own. He had already turned the engine on to work in tandem with the rudder that also moved freely and attempted to point the bow into the wind to hold his position. But the gusting winds and waves fought back harder than he could manage and rendered it entirely pointless.

Some three hours later, as the darkness slowly disappeared to make way for what little daylight the heavy clouds allowed through, Patrick was still battling to stay alive. Blood seeped from the open blisters across his palms where he had been fighting at the wheel to control the boat. But he barely felt it sting. His hands and entire body were near frozen. He had persisted with his calls for help, refusing to be beaten. Yet, to no avail.

Behind him, the waves seemed to have increased in size and he'd come dangerously close to capsizing more than once. He had chosen not to take count. It took every ounce of mental strength to stay hopeful. At one stage, he even prayed. He had somehow recalled a story he had once heard during one of the very few times his mother had dragged him off to church. A story of how Jesus had calmed a storm. He didn't know if he believed it, or if there was a God who created the very ocean he found himself in, but he had decided he'd at least try asking him for help.

But the storm was relentless, and as the new day broke to light up the entire ocean around him, he suddenly stared death full in its face.

It only took the enormous force of one last wave to capsize the yacht.

CHAPTER FOUR

Adam glanced at the news reporter's face on the television as he stumbled inside from the storm. The mood at The Lighthouse was somber—and with good reason. Even though the small principal building was entirely constructed from brick and mortar and fairly safe from storms, none of them had slept much the night before. Most of the mission team were in town helping at the shelters and he, Daniel, Elsbeth, and Jim had stayed behind to keep watch over the rest of the mission's dwellings that weren't as sturdy against storms.

"She looks scared," Adam commented on the reporter who stood knee-deep in water under a strained umbrella. He hung up his wet coat before bending down to pat Cassie's furry head.

"I don't blame her," Elsbeth commented, handing him a towel. "How's it looking out there?"

"Not good, I'm afraid. Chief Perry says the river-bank might not hold if the rain persists. He's reinforced it as much as he could and has a team on standby, but it might not be enough."

He poured himself a cup of coffee and walked over to where Daniel sat watching the early morning news on the small black-and-white television.

"What's the latest?" he asked.

"They officially declared it a category one hurricane. Named it Hurricane Troy. Who comes up with these names?" Daniel said.

"Beats me. All I know is that Chief Perry has his hands full keeping the town safe. It's already done a lot of damage. I've just dropped off the last of our food parcels. Both shelters are packed to capacity. And if the banks blow, we're stuck here. The bridge won't be safe to cross."

Daniel got up, walked over to the window, and peered out through a small gap in the storm shutters.

"Let's just hope no one got caught in those waves last night. I don't think I've ever seen them quite this big. The tide's just about pushed in right up to our boundary. Looks like the wind got to the fence too. It might be a good idea for us to remove any loose pieces of debris before the wind picks it up."

Adam had joined Daniel at the window.

"Yeah, it's bad. I'll take a walk down with Jim as soon as he gets back. He's gone to fetch some more sandbags to put outside the church."

They turned their attention to the TV where a wind-blown weather girl was reporting live from one of the nearby towns.

"Floods continue across the East Coast as Hurricane Troy swept into the port city of Wilmington late last night. While it hit land as a tropical storm it has now reached the low category one hurricane status with wind speeds already reaching upwards of seventy-five miles per hour in some locations. We expect it to strengthen and increase by tomorrow morning. Predictions show however that it should run out of steam and weaken by tomorrow evening. People are urged to remain sheltered until local authorities have cleared any threat of storm surge in your local areas before returning home."

Daniel dropped back down in his lounge chair.

"Well, that's glorious news, isn't it? Looks like Troy will soon blow over." He laughed at his clever play on words.

"I'd get some shuteye if I were you, Daniel. I reckon many of our community members might need some prayer and encouragement after the storm has settled. Chief Perry says most of the houses along the beach-front have been hit hard by the winds. I am fairly certain we are going to have several residents query God's hand in this."

Adam turned to grab his coat from the hook behind the door.

"Where are you going? You haven't slept a wink all night, Adam," Elsbeth said in her typical maternal fashion.

"Jim's most likely back with the bags by now. He'll need a hand. The quicker we offload the sandbags, the quicker we can get down to the fence to check how it's holding up before the winds get out of hand. That tide's also pushing awfully close to our property lines."

Daniel shifted to the edge of his seat, preparing to get up.

"And where do you think you're going?" Elsbeth stopped him midway.

"You heard the man, Elsbeth. Jim's going to need some help with those sandbags. He's not getting any younger."

"And neither are you. Besides, I'm not staying here on my own."

"She's right, Daniel. With the rest of the team helping at the shelters in town, she'd be here alone. Best you stay behind with Elsbeth. I'll shout if I need help."

Daniel lifted his hands above his head and shifted back in his chair.

"Fine, fine, I won't argue. Just promise you'll be

careful out there, okay? According to this young woman, the worst is still to come."

WHEN ADAM ARRIVED AT THE CHURCH WHERE THEY HAD expected Jim to have already turned up, there was no sign of him or his truck. Inside the church, the wind had swept debris against one of the small windows that lined the top of the wall where it met with the ceiling and had blasted the glass across the floor. Bibles and hymn sheets lay strewn between the pews and throughout the church. He scooped several Bibles up and secured them inside one of the band's instrument trunks atop the small stage before he turned back to fetch more. When he had finished putting all of them away, he stuck his head outside the door to look for Jim, but he still hadn't arrived. It wasn't like him to dawdle somewhere or be this late without letting them know.

He reached for the phone on the wall to call him when Daniel suddenly burst through the doors behind him.

"Jim's in trouble, Adam. Come quick!"

"Why, what happened?" Adam responded as he and Daniel started making their way toward the main building.

"I'm not sure. He called in on the office phone, but I couldn't quite make out what he was saying—the line was too scratchy. All I heard was *help* and *bridge*."

"You don't think the bridge collapsed do you?"

"No idea. Elsbeth is trying to get hold of the chief as we speak. But there's no time to wait for them to arrive. We're going to have to go look for him."

"You're right. Elsbeth will have to brave it alone for the time being. She'll be fine with Cassie keeping watch by her side. Besides, we need someone to man the phone in case he calls again."

"We'll take my car," Daniel said, already getting behind the wheel.

They drove along the single-lane coastal road to where it would eventually meet up with the narrow bridge they'd need to cross to get into town. There was no sign of Jim anywhere. While Daniel drove, Adam tried calling Jim's mobile several times.

"It just goes straight to voicemail."

"Keep calling. It might just be a momentary drop in the signal," Daniel said, battling to keep their vehicle from being pushed off the road by the strong wind.

But after several more attempts and still no answer, Adam was worried.

Lord, keep watch over Jim, please. Keep him safe.

"He'll be just fine, Adam. Our Father looks after his children," Daniel said as if he had read Adam's mind.

A second later Adam's mobile rang. It was Elsbeth.

"I got hold of the firehouse. Chief Perry's got two of his men heading to the town's side of the bridge."

"Great job, Elsbeth. We're about a minute away from the bridge on our end. Keep the line free just in case Jim tries to call again."

Elsbeth agreed and hung up.

It took longer than a minute to reach the bridge in the gusty wind. They had brought their vehicle to a standstill and got out to search on foot. Armed with a spotlight, they shone its light across the bridge, hoping to find Jim's truck, but there was no sign of it. They took turns calling out Jim's name but the wind carried their voices away the instant the sound left their throats.

"It's useless!" Daniel yelled back at Adam where he continued shouting. "Even if he hears us, we won't be able to hear him call back! Let's split up on both sides of the road and then cross the bridge!"

Adam put his thumb up to signal that he agreed.

On either side of the road, the ground sloped down toward the banks of the torrential river that flowed underneath the bridge. Some walls further along the river had already fallen away under the strong current and heavy downpour. Even with the sun up, the dark gray clouds and heavy rain made it nearly impossible to see clearly, and Adam strained his eyes as the wind and rain hit his face. Satisfied his side of the road was clear, he turned around to meet up with Daniel, who stood waiting for him at the start of the bridge.

"Anything?" Adam asked when he joined him.

"Nothing. I say we carefully make our way across the bridge on foot. I don't think we should put the bridge under unnecessary strain with the weight of the car. It looks pretty unstable down there," Daniel replied.

About ten yards onto the bridge where they'd been walking on opposite sides of the road along the railings, it was Daniel who spotted Jim's car first.

"Adam! Over here!" He flashed his torch to grab his attention.

In the distance they saw Jim's truck sideways across the road, its nose buried into the railing of the bridge. As they ran towards him, Adam yanked Daniel back when he reached to open the passenger side door.

"No, Daniel! Don't!" He pointed to where the truck's front wheels hung precariously just over the edge of the bridge.

Behind the steering wheel, Jim sat frozen in his seat, his body pushed back against the truck's rear window, his eyes closed. He hadn't seen them yet.

"Jim!" Adam yelled to get his attention, but it took both him and Daniel to shout together before Jim heard them and opened his eyes, his head still pinned against the window behind him.

"We've got you, Jim! Hang on!" Adam yelled.

"I have a tow strap in the trunk. I'll go get it!" Daniel announced as he spun around and headed back to his car.

"Jim! Stay as still as you can. Daniel's coming back

with a tow rope. We'll get you out in no time!" Adam shouted moments before a gust of wind whipped underneath the truck and threatened to lift it over the bridge. The metal groaned as it screeched against the bridge's metal railing.

Don't let him go like this, Lord. Help us!

CHAPTER FIVE

I t seemed like all time had gone by when Daniel finally made it back to the scene of the accident, tow rope in hand.

The two men quickly tied one end around the iron guard rails on the opposite side of the bridge before securing the other end to Jim's truck.

"Be careful, Daniel!" Adam cautioned as another gust of wind blew toward them and threatened to lift Jim's truck over. But Daniel had already successfully snapped the hook onto the truck's towing hitch. The strap tightened as the truck's nose dipped forward over the edge of the bridge like a seesaw.

Adam gripped both hands around the strap and heaved back as if he were in a tugging war. Behind him, Daniel had already started tightening the ratchet. The metal rails groaned under the strain.

When they were certain it would hold up, Adam slipped around to the driver's side where Jim had remained in the precise position he had first found him.

Adam peered through the window, but the rain made it hard to see.

"Are you injured?" he shouted.

Jim didn't call back. He merely shook his head in the gentlest of ways.

"Undo your seatbelt!"

Jim's startled sideways glance instantly told Adam that he'd slip forward if he did so.

Adam ran back to where Daniel was guarding the ratchet.

"We need to pull it back more!" he shouted.

"I'm not sure we can! The railing is already bending."

"Do you have any more rope so we can disperse the weight?"

"No!"

Unsure of what to do next, Adam's eyes darted back to the truck.

"What if we lightened the load at the back, take off a few sandbags?"

"It's too risky! It might be the very thing that's keeping it from tipping over!"

Daniel was right. The weight of the sandbags had most probably been what initially prevented Jim from going over.

Adam paused for the briefest of moments before he yelled back to Daniel.

"When I give you the signal, work the ratchet as much as it allows!"

"Whatever you're planning, Adam, be careful! There's no taking chances now, son," Daniel cautioned, his voice trailing in the wind.

"I don't see any other way! We'll have to be quick, so wait for my signal!"

Back at Jim's side, Adam slowly opened the car door, careful not to shift the truck's weight. While he looked back at Daniel to assess if he was ready, he reached in and told Jim to grab hold of his arm. Jim did, albeit initially with a bit of trepidation.

"I got you, Jim. We have the car secured with a tow strap, but the railing won't hold if another gust comes. When I tell you to, unclip your seatbelt and jump towards me. We'll have to be quick, got it?"

Jim gave a gentle nod.

"It will be okay, Jim."

Adam tightened his grip around Jim's arm, aware of Jim's big hand doing the same around his.

"Ready?"

Again Jim nodded.

Adam's eyes met Jim's before he looked across to where Daniel was waiting for his signal.

"Now!" he yelled, signaling both Daniel and Jim simultaneously.

In one perfectly coordinated second, Jim unclipped his seat belt while Daniel worked the ratchet and Adam yanked Jim's body from the truck, moments before another gust of wind swept across the bridge.

The blustering wind whipped beneath the truck, lifting the rear of the vehicle and shifting the nose further forward over the edge of the bridge. Behind the truck, the strain on the ratchet was too much, and it exploded into a dozen pieces, one of which slammed into Daniel's forehead, leaving a blood-streaked gash in its place. There was no stopping the truck as it took mere seconds for the nose to tip over before it pulled the rest of the truck over the side of the bridge where it came to a thundering crash in the fast-flowing river below.

On the tarmac next to where the truck had been mere moments ago, Jim and Adam lay shielding their heads.

"Are you okay?" a male voice echoed in the distance.

A few moments later, two fire and rescue fighters dropped to their knees beside them.

"We sure are," Adam replied with a thankful heart.

"She's not going to hold, fellas. We need to get you out of here," one announced just as the bridge shuddered beneath them.

"We have our car just beyond the bridge! We'll be fine, but you'd better get on out of here!" Adam warned as the start of a large crack in the road behind them warned of what was imminent.

"We have our orders, Pastor Adam, let's go!"

"You'll be left stranded at The Lighthouse if the bridge collapses. You're more needed in town. Go on!"

"Copy that, Pastor! Godspeed!" one said as they turned and ran back to the other end of the bridge.

As the group of men split up to make their way back to the opposite ends of the bridge, the bridge groaned noisily beneath their feet. It didn't take long before the plates shifted and the entire bridge tilted to one side. By now Adam, Jim, and Daniel had picked up the pace and had just made it back to their car when they turned around to watch the piece of the bridge closest to them collapse into the water below, leaving a gaping hole behind.

Bit by bit the bridge crumbled as if it were a cookie that had soaked in a cup of coffee for too long. Beneath it, the rushing river swept some of the broken chunks away while the larger pieces sank to the bottom and disappeared for good.

Across the way, they watched as the two fire and rescue men got back to their truck moments before the rest of the bridge slowly dropped into the water between them.

"If that wasn't a narrow escape, then I don't know what is. Are you okay?" Adam asked once Jim settled into Daniel's car.

"The old knee's a bit sore, but I'll be fine," Jim responded, still out of breath.

"You did okay for an old man, Jimmy." Daniel broke the tension.

"Says he who's practically the same age," Adam laughed. "I say I should get both of you golden oldies back in Elsbeth's caring hands asap."

AS EXPECTED, ELSBETH STOOD READY WITH DRY TOWELS and a hearty pot of chicken soup she had defrosted the night before.

"Who would have known frozen chicken soup could taste this good," Daniel said as he dished out a second helping.

"Best I've ever had, thank you, Elsbeth," Jim agreed as he got up to grab his raincoat.

"Well, all the chicken soup in the world won't fix that limp so you can hang that coat right back, Jim. You're hardly in any position to be out there," Elsbeth stopped him.

"She's right, Jim. You nearly died back there. You should take it easy with that knee of yours," Adam said.

"Not to be difficult, Adam, but the wind's pushing in from the ocean and I'm pretty sure the debris has hit the cabins along the fence," Jim reasoned.

"Adam and I will go check on the fence and the cabins, Jimmy. You've already busted that knee of yours once. With the bridge out, there's no way we can get you to the hospital if you bust it a second time."

Jim couldn't deny the fact that his body currently felt every inch its retirement age.

"In that case, I'll have another bowl of that delicious soup of yours please, Elsbeth."

Adam turned the volume on the TV up when the broadcast switched to the meteorologist reporting.

"News just in from the National Hurricane Center. We expect the wind speed to increase to the maximum category one speed as measured by the Saffir-Simpson scale. With wind speeds expected to reach up to ninety-five miles per hour earlier than initially anticipated, we are now facing the possible start of a category two storm. We have been told that this storm has proven to be quite unpredictable, and we urge you to make sure you are properly prepared for the storm which is expected to worsen by as early as tonight."

Daniel snorted.

"So much for Hurricane Troy blowing over. I say we had better get down to those cabins and see if we can get ahead of this thing before it's too late," Daniel said, already buttoning his coat.

"Right behind you," Adam responded.

He paused at the door and looked back at Elsbeth.

"I'm sure the two fellows on the bridge already informed Chief Perry, but it might not be a bad idea to touch base with him about the bridge being out. Until the wind dies down and a helicopter can reach us, we're stuck here."

Adam patted Cassie's head and told her to take care of Elsbeth and Jim until they got back.

"We'll be fine. It's you I'm worried about," Jim said.

"You should take a walkie-talkie… just in case you need help," he added. Elsbeth rummaged through a nearby drawer and handed him one of the two-way radios, linking the channel with one she held back.

THE TWO MEN FOUGHT THEIR WAY THROUGH THE SHEETS of rain and gusts of wind that had already increased substantially since they got back from rescuing Jim. Tree branches and scattered foliage lay blasted across the communal lawns, forcing them to navigate their way with caution. With their heads bowed, hoping to protect their faces from the pelting rain that felt more like bullets slamming against their skin, they soon reached the first of the cabins along the lower end of the property boundary. The door had been blown off and half the roof had caved in from an enormous pile of debris that had been forced there by the wind.

Along one of the outer walls, the mutilated bodies of about a dozen seagulls lay on the ground where they had met their deaths as the wind smashed them into the timber exterior. It was a ghastly sight that resembled something from a Hitchcock movie.

There were no words exchanged between the two men as they moved between the badly damaged cabins. There was no need. The storm had left its mark and there was no stopping it now. When they reached the perimeter fence, the wind had also knocked that over in several places and the two men soon stared at the entangled display of wire half buried in the sand.

"It's no use, Adam. He's already dead," Daniel said when Adam lifted a pile of tangled wire away to reach a stray cat that had gotten caught in the mess. The feline was no stranger to them. He had taken up residence at The Lighthouse some time back and frequently hovered around the kitchen for scraps. But he was never really tame enough to allow anyone close to him. They had named him Phantom because of his shiny gray coat and elusive nature.

All creatures great and small, the Lord God loves them all. The words rang in Adam's head as he scooped several hands of sand to cover it up.

"Tell me you're also seeing that!" Daniel suddenly cried out behind him.

"What?"

"That! There!"

As Adam straightened next to Daniel and allowed his eyes to follow his pointed finger to a spot where the stormy waves crashed onto a nearby rocky cove along the coastline, he saw it too.

CHAPTER SIX

Their feet hit the uneven sand almost in tandem as they ran towards the rocky edge of the inlet. Waves crashed against their legs where the water pushed up to swallow the remaining bit of beach while the strong wind threatened to blow them off their feet. Forced to hold on to each other, they powered against the elements, all the while keeping their eyes pinned on the object they hadn't quite fully digested yet.

When they eventually reached it, and their eyes won the war against the attacking rain, there was no mistaking it.

They stared at the yacht's giant white underbelly that had come to a crashing halt against the rocks—its upside-down nose wedged firmly between the boulders, pushing further onto the rocks with every approaching wave. The mast had been entirely broken off and rendered the yacht fully upside down. Floating to one side was the remains of a tattered mainsail and its tangled rig that must have gotten dragged through the ocean along the way. Adam and Daniel watched in horror as their eyes settled on the luminous yellow pile that had somehow stayed atop the wrong-side-up boat wreck. It didn't take them long to determine that they had laid eyes on a man—a survivor.

"Hello!" Adam yelled out first.

"Can you hear me? Hello!"

The man didn't move.

Daniel had already made his way up and over the jagged rocks toward the bow in the hopes of there being a way he could climb up to him, but it proved impossible.

"I'll have to try getting up from the stern," Daniel reported.

"Impossible! It's halfway underwater. One wrong wave along with bad timing and you'll get slammed into those sharp rocks."

"We have to do something, Adam. For all we know, he's still alive."

While Adam agreed they couldn't leave him there, he just couldn't quite wrap his head around how anyone could've survived at sea in as bad a storm as this one.

His hands were already working at taking off his shoes when he said, "I'll do it. Radio Jim and have him contact the Coast Guard."

Daniel didn't argue. Adam had been surfing off the cove since puberty and if anyone knew how to navigate their way across those rocks, it'd be him. Turning his back against the storm, he called for Jim over the two-way radio.

"Jimmy, come in please, over."

It took no time at all before Daniel heard Jim's reply.

"Receiving you loud and clear, Danny, over."

"We got ourselves a capsized yacht on the rocks by the cove. There's a man. Not sure yet if he's alive, he's tied himself to the underbelly of the boat. Adam's trying to get to him, but you'd best get hold of the Coast Guard and see if they're able to reach us."

"Copy that, Danny. Over and out."

When Daniel ended the call, he saw Adam had already maneuvered his way along the rocks to the stern where he was hanging onto the boarding ladder that was below the turbulent waterline. Behind him, another wave rushed closer and Daniel caught himself holding his breath and curling his toes as if he was ready to climb the boat himself before the wave smashed into it. But Adam knew never to turn his back on the sea and had already prepared to rock climb his way to the rudder that had miraculously stayed intact. His feet left the water mere seconds before another powerful wave crashed into the back of the boat, followed by a forceful gust of wind. The motion nearly caused him to lose his balance, but he held on and used the momentum to swing his body onto the hull of the boat, grabbing hold of the rudder with one hand.

His bare feet slipped on the smooth surface when he tried to regain his balance. Standing wasn't an option. Challenged by the relentless rain and gusty winds, it was impossible to walk along the edge of the hull. Instead, he took up position on his belly as if he were on his surfboard, and carefully slid along the boat's framework, pulling and pushing his body into motion like a centipede. With his head up and eyes focused on the body directly ahead of him, it took just about all his muscle power to navigate his way along the base of the yacht. When he finally reached the keel where the man had cleverly attached himself to the fin-like structure, he paused to catch his breath while he searched for any signs of life.

But the man didn't move. His body was in a similar position—flat on his belly, arms and legs draped over the sides of the boat like a starfish.

"Hey, can you hear me?" Adam called out, but the body didn't move.

The sudden realization that he might not have survived the storm tugged at Adam's insides. He pulled his body into a semi-seated position, holding onto the keel, so he could reach out and touch the man's bare feet in front of him. But he couldn't bring himself to do it. The man's feet were a horrible purplish color. Too much water exposure had shriveled up his skin, and there were several open cuts on one of them. He allowed his eyes to work their way up to the man's hands, which looked much the same as his feet. Adam couldn't see his face. It was buried beneath the oversized raincoat's large hood. Somewhat ashamed, Adam caught himself being relieved that he couldn't see it. He was pretty certain it would mirror the same deep purple hues of his limbs.

When another gust of wind smashed the rain into the side of Adam's face, he snapped out of his trance as if it was God who'd smacked him back to reality. It worked, and Adam found his hand almost instantly reach out to touch one of the man's motionless legs. Again he called out to the man whose body still hadn't reacted to his touch, but Adam was almost certain he had heard a moan. He shuffled his body closer until his feet touched the man's, ignoring the strange sensation he got from them in return.

Adam's hand worked its way along the bright orange lanyard that had been twisted and tied around the keel to where the other end was secured around the man's midriff. When he eventually wedged four of his fingers between the cord and the man's waist, he gave it a gentle but firm tug. In an instant, the man's body responded with a strained groan.

"Hey! You're alive," Adam responded in elation.

"He's alive!" he yelled to Daniel, who stood patiently waiting for feedback on the rocks below.

"Wake up, man. You're safe now. We're going to get you out of here," Adam said, his fingers still tugging at the man's waist.

The man groaned once more, his body still sprawled out and unmoving.

"It's okay, buddy. Just stay still. I'll have you down in a jiffy."

But Adam knew it wouldn't be quick, or easy.

He'd have to swing the man over the edge of the boat and hope that the lanyard extended far enough to deposit the survivor into Daniel's arms. But a quick assessment soon revealed that it wouldn't reach all the way—at least not while still tied to the keel. It meant that he'd have to untie the cord at the keel and rely on his physical strength alone to lower him onto the rocks, running the risk of losing his own grip and falling onto the treacherous rocks below.

Dear Lord, I can't do this. I'm not strong enough.

But as soon as he sent the words up to the heavens, God replied with one of his favorite scriptures.

"He gives strength to the weary and increases the power of the weak."

And while Adam knew full well the reference wasn't to physical strength, he rested knowing that God would renew his mind to believe that his body was physically capable of it.

With body, mind, and soul aligned in faith, he began untying the cord behind him. When his cold and wet fingers fumbled with the last knot, he readied his body for the survivor's weight. Still seated with his legs pulled up and squeezing the boat's frame between his thighs as if he were sitting on a horse, he gently released the lanyard inch by inch.

"You ready, buddy? If you can grip onto the boat at any stage, please feel free." His voice was light and almost comical. A feeble attempt to keep himself sane in the moment.

But the man's body remained flaccid and unresponsive.

"It's up to you and me, Daniel!"

"Ready when you are, Adam. Take it as slow as you need to!"

Using his lower back to secure the rope while one hand curled in a firm grip around the cord, Adam squeezed his thighs tighter into the boat's frame. Freeing his other hand, looking much like he was riding a bull in a rodeo, he gently lifted the man's leg and moved it over the boat to join his other leg. Expecting the man's body to tilt over and get dragged down by gravity, he heaved into the cord around his body.

But the man's body hardly budged an inch. It had been held in place—almost glued to the boat—by the rubbery fabric of the bright yellow raincoat.

So much so that at one stage Adam had to push one foot down on the man's shoulder to help it glide along the side of the boat, as if he had the suction pads of the very starfish he'd resembled mere moments ago.

Adam's lips curled into a smile. God knew this would happen.

Even the rain had momentarily eased off.

When, minutes later, the man's body neatly flopped onto Daniel's back, Adam praised God for his almighty providence, then descended the yacht the same way he had climbed up, pausing and waiting for a set of nasty waves to pass before his feet landed firmly on the rocks again.

He found Daniel on the beach where he had already set the man down on the highest patch of sand against a dune.

"How's he doing?"

"No idea. All I know is he's barely breathing," Daniel answered, still out of breath.

"It's hypothermia. We need to get him warm, and quickly."

But, with the man's head and face now visible, the hypothermia wasn't all that concerned them.

CHAPTER SEVEN

Most of the day had passed since the young man had washed ashore. Adam and Daniel had carried him to the safety of their shelter, where they had set him down near the fireplace on the only camping stretcher they had. They had dried him off and smothered his hypothermic body with blankets.

"You know he needs stitches," Elsbeth commented from where she sat next to Daniel when, for the fourth time in less than an hour, he needed to change the blood-soaked dressing on the gaping five-inch gash across their patient's head.

"Uh-huh. His body is warming up so the blood flow's returning to normal. At least he's still passed out. I would imagine this wound to be pretty painful. As long as he doesn't bleed out on us, he'll be okay until we can get him to the hospital."

"The hypothermia might just have saved his life. He could've bled out otherwise," Jim added.

"Any news from the Coast Guard?" Adam said, looking at Jim.

"Not since their last contact two hours ago, no. There's nothing they can do in this weather, Adam. The wind's just too strong for any of their helicopters to fly, and the sea's no safer. Chief Perry's already alerted the hospital in Wilmington but they have their hands full with storm surge victims. The bottom line is they're facing the same challenge with their medevac helicopter."

"Hurricane Troy's not letting up anytime soon, according to the latest news report either. If I can't stop this wound from bleeding, we could lose him," Daniel said as he finished up the fresh dressing.

"I have a sewing kit here somewhere. If I sterilize the needle and the wound, I'll have a stab at some temporary stitches. It won't be perfect, but if it worked in the war, it'll work now," Elsbeth said bravely.

Her suggestion resulted in blank stares from all three men.

She threw one hand on her hip. "What? I've done all the sewing around here for decades and none of y'all have ever complained."

"Well, Elsbeth, I think that if anyone can do it, you can. We should have a bottle of Doc Grady's moonshine in the pantry somewhere. He'd be thrilled to know his grandfather's secret recipe saved someone's life," Jim said.

"I agree. Go fetch your sewing kit, Dr. Porter. I'll go find the spirits," Daniel said in jest with an affectionate pat on her shoulder as he passed her.

"And that's my cue," Adam announced.

Jim chuckled.

"You've never had the stomach for these things, have you?"

"Afraid not, I'm feeling sick just thinking about Elsbeth driving a needle through the man's flesh. I'd rather go check his clothes to see if we can at least find out who the guy is—let his family know he's okay." He paused, then continued. "Let's just pray he was alone on that boat. I'd hate if he had a wife and—"

Adam didn't finish his sentence. It hadn't been that long since he lost Ruth and Abigail and the very thought that this man could've suffered the same pain killed him.

"I don't think he was married, Adam. He's not wearing a ring." Jim spoke gently. "He looks young. If I had to hazard a guess I'd say the fellow's about twenty-seven, at best. And with his rugged looks and obvious money judging by that fancy yacht, he's likely to be a bit of a ladies' man. Probably from upstate, but it would be good to know for sure." Jim jerked his chin toward the wall with the bathroom on the other side. "Elsbeth hung his clothes to dry in the shower."

Daniel and Elsbeth brushed past Adam as they re-entered the room.

"Everything okay?" Daniel enquired of Jim upon observing the look on Adam's face. He could read Adam like a book.

"Ah, he'll be fine. This thing's just scratching at some old wounds. Speaking of, I see you're all set for the operation."

"Hardly an operation, Jim," Elsbeth said, already disinfecting one of her needles.

"Well, I'm with Adam on this one. I can't watch." He turned his back toward them.

As if God heard his silent prayer for a better distraction, Adam, much to his surprise, returned. With one hand shielding his view of Elsbeth who had already started working on the survivor's wound, he quickly sat down on the sofa next to Jim.

"Back so soon?" Jim giggled.

But Adam didn't answer. He was far too engrossed in the item in his hand.

"From that look on your face, I'm guessing you found something. What you got there, son?" Daniel said over his shoulder, commenting on the watertight pouch in Adam's hands.

"Not sure yet, I found it clipped to the inside of his rain jacket."

"Did you find anything else?" Jim asked.

"Only a sat phone, but I think you are spot on, Jim.

The guy's clothes are expensive designer labels. Certainly not labels you find around here."

"Well, go on then, open the pouch," Daniel urged as he dabbed at a fresh pool of blood between Elsbeth's stitches.

When several moments later Adam had said nothing, Daniel urged again.

"And? What is it?"

"Other than it being a leather-bound notebook with hundreds of numbers, I don't have a clue."

"Numbers? Like phone numbers?" Elsbeth said, keeping her eyes and mind focused on the job at hand.

"No, I don't think so. At least not any area codes I recognize. It's quite odd looking, actually."

"Well, it has to mean something for him to have chosen that over his wallet," Jim said.

"I guess we'll have to ask him when he wakes up. Not that it's any of our business, really. I was just hoping it would tell us more about who he is and where he's from."

As if on cue, the young man let out a barely audible moan.

Elsbeth paused as she pulled tight the thread of a stitch, her face scrunched up in anticipation of him waking.

"You'd better hurry with those stitches before he wakes up, Elsbeth," Daniel whispered.

"Hold him down, just in case," she whispered in return.

But the moment the needle touched the man's skin again, he groaned, and this time, he attempted to move his head though even with his eyes still closed, it was obvious he wasn't quite lucid yet.

"Keep going," Daniel advised Elsbeth, who had now paused midway between stitches.

"Oh, I don't know, Daniel. Maybe I should stop. It's too painful for him."

"You can't stop now, Elsbeth. Keep going," Daniel said, surprised at her sudden lack of courage to continue.

"It was easier when I knew he couldn't feel anything," she confessed, her face still pulled into an empathetic frown.

"Would you rather he bleed out? He's not fully awake yet, so crack on. Hurry."

As always, Daniel was right, so Elsbeth drew in a deep breath and continued. This time, their patient's body reacted with force to the pain.

"Whoa, young man. You'd best keep still. We're almost done. You've got a nasty cut across your head. Hang in there." Daniel tried to settle him down, raising his eyebrows and lifting his chin to signal that Elsbeth should keep going.

It took four more stitches and several agonizing moans before Elsbeth was finally done. The instant she cut the thread after the last stitch, she fled the room in tears, leaving Daniel to tend to the stranger on his own.

"There now, we're done," Daniel said as he wiped a moonshine-doused cotton ball along the cut and applied a fresh dressing.

"That should do it, young man. I can't guarantee your sharp haircut will remain intact, but Elsbeth's done a pretty neat job of stitching you up. She's not one who enjoys hurting people—found it easier when you were asleep, but without her courage, you might have bled to death. You're okay now. Here, take these." He popped two painkillers in the young man's mouth and chased it down with a glass of water, which he eagerly gulped half of before dropping his head back down on the pillow.

It was the first time the newcomer had opened his eyes fully. Filled with questions, he settled them on Daniel's face, but he didn't speak.

"I'm Daniel. What's your name?"

His lips parted to prepare for answering, but no words left his mouth. It was when his eyebrows drew a question mark across his face that Daniel instantly suspected something was wrong.

"Where are you from, buddy?"

Again a puzzled look met Daniel's question.

"It's okay, lad. Take your time. You've been through a lot. You miraculously survived a category one hurricane at sea. But we'll talk more when you're stronger. You just need to rest for now."

The young man didn't have the strength to fight and almost instantly fell asleep again.

"You think he'll be okay?" Elsbeth directed at Daniel when she returned and took a seat next to Adam.

Daniel shrugged his shoulders and raised his eyebrows as he wiped his hands on a cloth.

"No way of knowing really, I guess time will tell. You did an outstanding job on those stitches though, well done. I know it was tough, but without them, I'm pretty certain he wouldn't have made it through the night. At least now we have a chance. You did good." He smiled from his seat in one of the chairs nearby where Adam and Jim sat poring over the notebook.

"Perhaps we should call up Doc Grady and see what he recommends we do now. He looks really pale," Elsbeth said.

"His body has been through a lot. He's lost a lot of blood and he nearly died of hypothermia. And only God knows how long he's been out there fighting to stay alive. I reckon his pale complexion is pretty normal considering," Jim said.

Elsbeth glanced at Adam where he sat with his elbows on his knees, studying the little oxblood-colored notebook he had found earlier.

"You're very quiet," she said. "Why the frown?"

They watched as Adam ran his thumb through the pages.

"I'm not sure what to make of this. I mean, of all the things he could've chosen to keep safe, he picks this. No wallet, no ID, no photos, nothing. Not even a cell phone, just this. Am I the only one who's finding it strange?"

"Perhaps he had his wallet or a phone in his pocket and lost it when he fell into the water. Who knows?" Daniel speculated as he leaned in over Adam's shoulder.

Adam allowed the possibility to take shape in his mind, but in his gut, he recognized the stirring that was also taking shape. There was no denying the warning signals that threatened to push all common sense aside. Those numbers meant something. Something that had this stranger choose to protect it no matter what.

CHAPTER EIGHT

B orn into his father's empire, William Sutton, Jr., was every bit a privileged trust fund baby. Raised amongst the New York elite, he had graduated summa cum laude from Harvard Medical School—even though it was only to appease his father.

The tabloids had pinned William's achievement on the fact that his father's company owned America's largest private healthcare network. A hugely successful company that also made regular sizable donations to the university and hosted just about any and every charity event known to humanity.

It then came as no surprise that despite having obtained his infamous qualification, William hadn't spent a single day in any of his father's hospitals. In part because his heart was never in it, but mostly in rebellious retaliation against his father's control over his life.

Instead, he chose to take full advantage of his family trust fund. A fund he legally gained access to the day he turned twenty-five.

Once a week, however, he attended the habitual board meeting for the sake of keeping his father happy, and his trust fund active, which was the only proviso of his contract. He was the youngest member on the Gencorp Holdings board and, to the rest of the board members, greatly equipped and invested in the company's interests. He did his utmost pretending to show an interest in the company that was due to one day be his but, truth be told, William knew he'd never meet his father's high expectations of running his company—even though he had been groomed to take over from his father—if that moment ever came—since the day he was born. The great Dr. Bill Sutton had long since passed retirement age yet had no plans of stepping down anytime soon; the biggest bone of contention between them.

And so, when William wasn't making a virtue of necessity at Gencorp, he spent the rest of his time frequenting an exclusive Country Club in Staten Island, showing no regard for the thirty-mile commute his driver had to make in peak traffic most days of the week. All in the name of a sixty-minute game of tennis or a fun round of nine-hole golf before a leisurely lunch with his entitled friends.

At night he was a regular at several of New York's

finest restaurants and nightclubs, where he would occasionally avail himself of illegal stimulants, something he said he needed in order to add more spice to his life. As if his luxurious socialite lifestyle lacked for anything. Truth be told, it was William's way of escaping the daily pressures of being the perfect son his father always wanted and he would never be. Instead, he was the son who was heir on paper but who'd never be good enough to take over his father's precious empire.

Until yesterday, when Dr. William (Bill) Sutton, Sr., had met his untimely fate and William inherited the entire Gencorp Holdings overnight.

The news had hit the tabloids almost as soon as the police had arrived at the scene, presumably leaked by one of the servers who had grabbed the opportunity to make a quick bonus. Photos of Bill's bloodied corpse—evidently taken with a mobile phone—had gotten displayed on just about every newspaper's front page that morning. They had called him a local hero who had saved millions of lives with his ground-breaking hospital technology and personal attention to the healthcare industry. Survived by his ailing wife and their only son, they had written that his death was a tragedy to all Americans.

WILLIAM'S TENNIS SHOES SQUEAKED NOISILY ON THE oatmeal-colored marble floors of his expensive penthouse apartment on Central Park South. His ordinarily fair complexion was abnormally pale as he now anxiously paced the large space. Tiny beads of sweat pearled along his hairline and threatened to run into his thick brows that took on the same strawberry blond color as his curly hair. With one freckled hand over his mobile, he pinned the device to his ear, waiting for his call to be answered while the other hand swept back and forth through his wavy hair.

"You were supposed to take care of it," he said into the phone through gritted teeth.

An answer came back.

"I don't care! Find it!"

He threw the phone across the floor, watching it splinter into several pieces before he took up his stance in front of the floor-to-ceiling window that overlooked Central Park. His hands trembled in anger—or was it fear?—by his hips.

After his father's body had been discovered during the charity dinner the night before, he had been by his mother's bedside until the police had allowed the guests to leave their home in the early hours of the morning. His parents had moved away from the city and took up permanent residence in the Hamptons almost immediately after his mother had fallen ill nearly six years prior. It had been a challenging time after her second failed kidney transplant and his father thought the tranquility and fresh air would be better for her overall health while they waited for a new donor kidney.

With a concierge medical team his father had personally selected and paid for, his mother was in expert hands while William met with the board and handled the press.

But so far things hadn't quite gone the way William had planned. With his mind still fully occupied by the cell phone conversation that had left him in such a state, the shrill tone of the telephone on the wall behind him startled him back into the present.

He lifted the receiver and barked at the caller.

"What?"

It was the doorman, telling him that the front of the building was crawling with paparazzi and news reporters and that he'd sent his driver round the back of the building instead.

"Vultures! My father's body is barely cold. I'll be right down." He paused before adding, "Sorry I snapped at you, Jo. It's just a lot to deal with right now."

When the call ended, he reached inside a nearby drawer to retrieve a new mobile phone. Since his temper had gotten the better of him several times before, he made sure to always have two spares on hand. He walked over to the broken Blackberry on the floor, popped the sim card from its slot, and slipped it and the battery into the new device. His new phone lit up like a slot machine as one by one the emails and text messages came through. He cursed under his breath when he read one of them. Choosing to ignore it, for now, he buried the phone in his pocket, quickly checked his image in the mirror, and rolled his Louis Vuitton luggage into the private elevator behind him.

Before the elevator reached the basement where he was due to meet his driver at the back exit, his phone rang.

"Sutton," he answered, not recognizing the number.

"Dr. Sutton, Detective Kane, NYPD Homicide."

"Yes?"

"I'm outside. Can we talk, please?"

"What more is there to talk about, Detective? I've told all I know to the police last night."

"I have a few more things I'd like to clarify, please."

"Look, it's not a great time. I have to get back to my mother and I'm late for a meeting with the board. Can this wait?"

"I'm afraid not, Dr. Sutton. It's important we inter-view all the... everyone as soon as possible."

"All the what? Suspects? You think I'm a suspect now?"

"It's just procedure, Dr. Sutton, until we have all the facts. Look, this place is teeming with press. I'm across the street, they haven't spotted me yet, but I think it goes without saying that it'll be better if they don't get wind of me being here. That'll open up a whole lot of opportunity for them to go crazy, if you know what I mean. Either I come up, or you meet me down at the station, your choice."

William scoffed.

"Well, that sounds like an ultimatum, Detective Kane. I don't think your chief will be too happy when I—"

"He's fully aware and I will bring him in on the interview if you like, Dr. Sutton. It is police procedure to do more in-depth interviews."

William went quiet, clearly rattled by the detective's response.

"What shall it be, Dr. Sutton? Your place or mine?"

"Fine, I'm walking to my car as we speak. I'll meet you at the station."

He hung up before the detective had a chance to respond.

"Shall I drive you to the office, sir?" his driver asked as William slipped into the backseat of his luxury Jaguar.

"It'll have to wait, Vlad. Apparently, I have more questions to answer at the police station. Just keep it on the down-low, please. The last thing I need now is the press on my tail."

"I understand, sir."

Vlad had been William's personal driver and security detail since he was just a child. Son of a Russian immigrant, his loyalty went beyond the call of duty and he had resorted to taking a few extraordinary measures to get William out of trouble many times before.

"Is everything okay, sir?" he asked when he saw the worried look on William's face.

"You're a good friend, Vlad. But it's best you sit this one out, for the sake of your and your family's safety."

"I can help, sir. You know you can trust me."

"I know, Vlad. It's not that. Look, I can't talk about it. It's too dangerous and I don't want you to be implicated in anything just because you're loyal to me and our family. I'll figure it out. I'll be fine."

But behind his brave words, William wasn't convinced he had the situation under control. This time, he might have gone too far.

74

CHAPTER NINE

Detective Harry Kane listened as his boss cautioned him.

"I don't think I have to tell you to watch your words very carefully, Kane. The press is already all over this thing, and I don't need a call from the mayor because you have a hunch. Tread carefully and make sure you follow procedure to the tee. If he did it, we'll catch him, but it's got to be by the book or he walks. Got it?"

"He's guilty, Chief. There's something off with this guy, I'm telling you."

"To the tee, Kane!"

"Yes, Chief."

He turned and joined his partner where she was waiting for him outside the chief's office.

Detective Angela Jones had been his partner for almost five years now and they worked well together.

She had proven her worth as one of the city's top African American female detectives, a role she took very seriously after her brother got in the way of a gang shooting in their neighborhood. Since then, she'd been obsessed with bringing justice to the city. Jonesy, as Kane called her, also grounded him. Something his ex-wife was never able to do in the almost fifteen years of their marriage.

"Keep your head, Kane. We'll get him," she said, grabbing hold of his arm just before they entered the interview room. She had seen the look on her partner's face and knew all too well he was fighting hard to hold back his personal opinions. For reasons she didn't quite understand, Kane had a gripe with the entitled kids of New York whom he claimed seemed to get away with all things illegal just because they had trust funds and influential parents.

The door slammed noisily behind them as Kane took a seat opposite William. Jones stood to one side.

"You have a cheek to keep me waiting, Detective. This is ridiculous," William spat.

"Sorry," Kane said in an attempt to swallow his pride and play it cool.

He folded his hands over a folder he kept closed on the table between them.

"Well, make this quick, please, Detective. As I said, I have to meet with the board."

"Yes, about that. Am I correct in saying you stand to

inherit all your father's shares in Gencorp Holdings as well as all subsidiaries attached to your father's name?"

"Yes."

"Do you know what it's worth? Ballpark figure."

"Of course I do. I am a member of the board, Detective. I know the numbers."

"Indeed. Would you agree that it's a substantial inheritance?"

William's eyes narrowed.

"Dr. Sutton? Am I correct in saying that you are the sole heir to your father's entire portfolio and that it amounts to quite a large amount of money?"

"Where are you going with this, Detective?"

Kane didn't answer. They both knew he was trying to establish a motive.

William rose abruptly from his chair and leaned forward across the table, his palms spread to add bulk to his frame.

"I don't have to answer your questions, Detective. I cannot see how it applies to my father's murder. That is what you're meant to solve, correct?"

"Correct."

"Then I suggest you get on with it and find the man who murdered my father!"

"Please take a seat, Dr. Sutton. I'm just trying to do my job. These are merely routine questions necessary to gain more insight into what happened."

"Like heck they are! You're treating me like I'm a

suspect. As if I would murder my own father. Do you hear yourself, Detective? I want my lawyer. I know my rights and I'm not saying another word without my lawyer present."

William sat back down in his chair and crossed his arms, depicting the exact image of the spoiled brat Kane said he was.

"That is your right, Dr. Sutton. But, before we get your lawyer involved, just so you are aware, we've studied all the surveillance footage throughout the house and none of it seems to account for your whereabouts at the approximate time of the murder."

"So you think I did it? Because you can't see me amongst the more than two dozen guests that attended our dinner last night. Have you ever thought that perhaps I was in the gents, or checking up on my mother where you'll find there are no cameras? You would've known that if you were good at your job, Detective. Now get me my lawyer."

"That won't be necessary. You're not under arrest, Dr. Sutton. You're free to go. But please know that we're only following—"

"Yes, yes, procedure, I've heard it all before, Detective. I suggest you take your procedure and focus it on finding the actual killer. Now if you'll please excuse me, I have a funeral to arrange and a company to run."

"Thank you for coming in, Dr. Sutton," Jones said, hoping to keep things pleasant.

"Oh, one more thing, Dr. Sutton, if I may?" Kane said, not waiting for his consent.

"Would you by any chance know what happened to Mr. Phillips? Patrick Phillips, he's your friend and your father's portfolio manager, correct?"

Caught off guard by the question, William frowned.

"What do you mean? Did you not question him last night?"

Kane shook his head.

"Well, I haven't seen him. I remember spotting him flirting with one of the assistants, but that was the last time I saw him. I assumed he snuck off with her. He's never really been one for these dos. I can give you his number if you like?" He took out his mobile to find it.

"No, that's quite all right, thank you, Dr. Sutton. We've got it. It's just we haven't been able to get hold of him via his phone, so I thought perhaps you might have seen or spoken to him?"

"I'm not his babysitter, Detective Kane. And no, I haven't seen or spoken to him since last night."

"We'll pop round to his apartment, thank you, but if you do happen to see or hear from him, please have him call me." He handed over his business card and added as politely as he could, "Thank you for coming in."

William left without saying another word.

"He's hiding something," Kane said to Jones the moment William stepped into the elevator and the doors closed behind him.

"Yep, he knows something all right. He was far too quick to request that fancy lawyer of theirs and way too eager to have us chasing after his so-called best friend. But you handled him well, Kane. I'm proud of you." She smiled.

"I can't stand these entitled brats. You know, where I come from, hard work was what got you the accolades and credentials. Not daddy's power or money."

"Well, you played by the book and that's good. We've got him where we need him, on his toes. We know he's hiding something. What, we'll figure out. We'll keep a close eye on him in the meantime. Entitled brats slip up and when that happens, we'll be there."

"Let's see what we have on this Phillips guy and track him down. He's the only one completely unaccounted for during the party."

They walked back to their desks and flopped down in their chairs at opposite ends of an oversized wooden desk that had seen better days. Facing each other, Jones opened Phillips' file on her computer.

"Right, shoot, what do we know about him?" Kane asked, squeezing a bright green stress ball in one hand.

"Age twenty-seven, earned an MBA from Harvard Business, majoring in economics and finance at the top of his class. They've been friends since childhood, apparently went to the same schools and vacationed together in the Hamptons."

Kane grunted.

"Another entitled brat, great."

"Yeah, not quite. His parents weren't wealthy at all. He's legitimately bright and worked really hard in school—got straight A's, never got into trouble, captain of the track team, et cetera, et cetera. Seems like a good guy."

"Siblings?"

"Nope, only child. His father was a construction manager, died of cancer when he was sixteen. His mother died five years later, natural causes. She never got to see her son graduate. That's brutal."

"So where did all their money come from to keep up with the Joneses? No offense, Jonesy."

"None taken, I'm not related." She flashed a smile before she continued.

"Apart from taking out three mortgages on their home, they made friends with the right people, I guess. Did whatever they needed to keep their only child in the best schools. Phillips got a scholarship to Harvard, so that expense got taken care of. It says here some of his parents' debt got settled from his father's life insurance policy when he died, but apparently, Phillips took care of his mother and all the bills once he landed a job on Wall Street. The guy's done pretty well for himself."

"Any connections to Gencorp Holdings?"

"He owns Investo, a private wealth management company. GenCorp is one of his clients. I have to tell you, I can't see motive here, Kane."

"So why run?"

"Who says he ran?"

"We interviewed everyone that was at the party last night except him, Jonesy. Where is he, huh? He's hiding. Guilty people hide."

"I think you're wrong about him. But I'll give you the benefit of the doubt, nonetheless. I say we pop round to his apartment and ask him ourselves."

TWO HOURS LATER, THE TWO DETECTIVES PULLED INTO A curbside parking spot opposite Patrick Phillips' Manhattan apartment. The doorman reported he hadn't seen him since he left around lunchtime the previous day—all spiffed up in a designer suit, which according to him wasn't Mr. Phillips' usual attire. He was apparently quite a decent, humble man.

Kane flashed the search warrant requesting the doorman to allow them entry into Philips' apartment. Considering the high profile status of the case, the judge hadn't hesitated to issue one and cited it as 'reasonable suspicion'.

The doorman's telling of Patrick Phillips' humility was confirmed when Kane and Jones stepped inside his modest apartment. The furniture looked homely, like hand-me-downs from his parents, and the general ambiance throughout was cozy and relaxing.

"Not really what I would have imagined a Wall

Street bachelor's pad to look like," Jones commented as she inspected the small pile of magazines on the coffee table. "I mean, this guy reads Martha Stewart's magazine. Really?"

"He's a tidy one too. Looks more like my mother's house than an up-and-coming twenty-seven-year-old's. He's even doing his own laundry," Kane said.

"A man after my own heart," Jones joked.

"Too domesticated if you ask me, but what do I know? You women seem to like that."

"Just a manly man who's in touch with his female side, Kane. You just ain't it, my friend, and that's okay. You'll find your lid."

"No thanks, I'm done with women. Speaking of which, did we get the assistant's name he was seen with last night?"

"Not yet."

"Well, the guy hasn't been here at all," Kane concluded before placing a call to the office.

"Hey, can you place a trace on Phillips' mobile and patch it through, please?"

He hung up.

"Judging from the crochet pillows and fresh flowers, I don't think he's the type to slice a man's throat," Jones said.

"I see your point, yet the guy's missing, Jonesy."

A message bleeped on his phone, and he skimmed through it.

"Interesting."

"What is?"

"Let's hope Martha Stewart shared her tips on surviving prison in those magazines of his. Seems to me the guy might need them. As it happens, his phone was already entered into evidence last night. Officers found it in the shrubs just outside Bill Sutton's office in the Hamptons. Right outside the scene of the crime. Like I said Jonesy, the man ran. He murdered Bill Sutton in cold blood and fled through the patio doors. Still think the guy's innocent?"

CHAPTER TEN

I t was well into the night when a loud clapping noise on the roof woke first Adam, then Daniel. They had all fallen asleep in their chairs after a failed attempt to keep watch over their nameless patient.

A few embers in the fireplace provided the only light in the room. Adam shuffled toward the window. Outside, the hurricane had weakened to a thunderstorm with lightning bolts that lit up the early morning sky. The wind had died down, but the rain had remained heavy.

"Sounds like Troy is slowly taking its leave," Daniel whispered from across the room where his fingers worked at the table lamp that had gone off. When it yielded no results he added, "Well, looks like the power's out."

"Possibly what that noise was atop the roof," Adam

replied. "I'll get the generator going as soon as the day breaks."

"I'll throw on some more logs, it's a bit nippy in here."

Adam's gaze moved to where the stranger was still sleeping on the nearby cot.

"You know, he could be a serial killer or a thief for all we know." He spoke quietly then asked, "Where do you think he came from?" His eyes were filled with suspicion.

"Only the good Lord knows, but does it really matter, son? I mean, the guy miraculously survived one of the worst storms this area has ever seen, and we found him." He chuckled. "He was practically handed to us. It's our Christian duty to help him. Who cares where he came from or who he is? We're Samaritans to all who need help."

Adam moved next to Daniel in front of the fire and added a log.

"It's not that though," he said in a whisper, as if he was about to share a secret. "He was brought to us for a reason. Nothing's a coincidence, that I know for certain. But with the bridge out and the storm still at it, we're trapped here, *with* him. He could be anyone, Daniel. That book, I can't shake it. Something is going on here."

The legs of the stretcher squeaked behind them, and they both turned to find the stranger sitting up in his bed.

"Where am I?" he said, his voice croaky.

It was Daniel who answered while Adam stood to one side, his arms wrapped around his body as if he was consoling himself with a hug.

"You're okay, buddy. You got caught in a hurricane at sea and your yacht capsized, washed up here in Turtle Cove. We run a mission, The Lighthouse. I'm Daniel and this is Adam, our pastor."

The orange glow from the fire revealed the confusion on his face.

"I can't remember any of it."

"That doesn't surprise me. You have a nasty cut across your head. What's your name?"

The man searched his mind.

"I… I don't know."

"Can you remember anything at all? Where you live, what work you do, anything?" Adam asked, his tone somewhat on edge. He got a panicked, blank stare from the stranger in response.

Daniel was quick to defuse the mood that had suddenly turned unpleasant.

"That's okay, lad. I'm sure your memory will return as soon as you get your strength back. You must be starving. It's a good thing we have a gas burner in the kitchen—the power's out. I'll go whip you up one of my special stacker sandwiches and a hearty glass of milk. My mother used to say, if it can turn a calf into a strong bull, it can turn a boy into a strong man. Not sure that's true, but hey, who am I to argue with my mother, huh?" Daniel chuckled as he prepared to leave the room, casting a silent warning in Adam's direction before he rounded the corner to the adjacent small kitchen.

In the moments that followed, while Jim and Elsbeth were still fast asleep, Adam fought hard to suppress the feelings of concern that threatened to overwhelm him. It troubled him to some extent. He used to be a trusting person. But ever since the accident and Carrie's kidnapping, he'd had a hard time trusting people. He'd spent hours in prayer asking God to restore his trust in people, sharpen his discernment, help him see the good in people again. But now he found himself staring at a stranger who couldn't seem to remember anything about himself or his life, and his stomach was in a tight knot.

He took a few steps back, then turned and walked over to the window. Perhaps it was something he did subconsciously to create distance between him and the stranger. He wasn't sure. All he knew was that he needed to control his raging emotions and take a moment to talk to God. He asked God to reveal the truth of this man's heart and have him see its substance through God's all-seeing eyes. Deep in thought, he peered at the storm outside and soon found himself deciding to take the first step in letting his guard down.

"The power's out," he started. "Probably just one of the cables that got hit by the lightning. It will be light within the hour though, the clouds are slowly lifting. I'll get the generator going so you can freshen up." He looked back and studied the stranger's frame. "I have some spare clothes that should fit you. Nothing as fancy as the ones you had on, but they'll do. At least the storm has settled down, so we should be able to get you to the hospital by air. They can run some tests and make sure you're okay."

His eyes rested on the man's boyish face. Jim was right. He looked to be in his late twenties, at most. His eyes told him he was as suspicious of them as he was of him. He looked afraid, uncertain. It tugged at Adam's heart, and in that moment he felt nothing but compassion for the man. Something he intuitively knew was God's doing. Allowing the Holy Spirit to take charge, Adam moved across the room and sat down on the edge of the sofa next to him.

"Hey, it's going to be okay." Adam's tone was gentle and reassuring. "My head hit a piece of coral once when I was out surfing at the reef, I was about fifteen. I couldn't remember much of anything either, but it all came back after a couple of days. I guess your body just needs a bit of time to recover. Besides, we're all praying for you." He finished with a smile.

The man's face blanked again.

"Do you know if you believe in God?" Adam asked with caution.

The man shrugged his shoulders and in that very moment, Adam found himself staring into the very depths of his soul. The man's eyes were warm and spoke of gentleness and kindness, not hatred or anything remotely evil. No more did this stranger know any of them than they knew him. Yet, he chose to blindly trust each of them. Whatever the circumstances that brought him to Turtle Cove, it didn't matter. What mattered was that God had purposed it all, and that was good enough for Adam. His trust didn't lie in man. His trust lay in the One who knew it all. And if God brought this young man to them, Adam knew with all his heart, mind, and spirit that it was for a good reason. And when the time came, God would reveal what was required of him and he'd know precisely what to do.

"Here we go, young man." Daniel entered with a sandwich stacked like the Tower of Babel. Proud of his culinary creation, he set it down in the man's lap, patting Cassie's head; she'd woken up to the smell of the freshly fried bacon.

"And that, my friend, is Daniel's favorite stack sandwich," Adam explained with an envious smile.

"Don't you fear, son." Daniel playfully wagged his index finger and smiled when he recognized the look on Adam's face. "I figured you'd want one too, so I've made enough for everyone. There are even some leftovers for old Cassie here." He wrapped his hands around the dog's ears and gave her head an affectionate massage.

"Tell me I'm not too late," Jim's half-asleep voice croaked from where he'd woken up on the sofa.

"You're eating without me?" said Elsbeth as she too sat up.

And as the storm steadily drifted away, the small group of friends welcomed the injured stranger into their lives and Turtle Cove. Ready to face whatever good work God intended.

"Now, how about we figure out what we're going to call our young survivor here? At least until we know his actual name," Daniel said as he disappeared into the kitchen and almost instantly returned with more stack sandwiches.

"Well, since he survived the raging seas that spat him out on our shore, I reckon we should call him Jonah," Jim suggested before digging into his breakfast.

Greeted with unanimous cheer, it was agreed and celebrated as if they had just welcomed a newborn to their family. All of which was well received by Patrick who, at that moment, felt a longing in his heart he couldn't explain. One that hinted towards a desperate need for something he didn't recall and wasn't entirely certain he had in his life. Something that said he belonged.

By midday, the medevac team had airlifted Patrick—or Jonah, as they had now named him—to the hospital in Wilmington. They had decided that Adam should accompany him to answer any questions about his medical status at the time of his rescue.

The nurses had wheeled him off to run a few scans while Adam stayed behind in the waiting area.

He mindlessly flipped through a few magazines before he headed to the café in search of some coffee. As he was waiting in line to be served, he glanced up at the television on the wall behind the counter. With the volume muted, he read the words on the right of the screen before his attention moved to a bright red banner that flashed across the bottom of the screen. It announced the tragic death of a man named Dr. Bill Sutton and made reference to his charity work and prominence in the medical industry. But it was the familiar image encased in a thick yellow frame with the word WANTED written below it that made Adam's heart sink to the pit of his stomach.

CHAPTER ELEVEN

The underground parking garage in a South Bronx neighborhood was eerily quiet and made William's pulse quicken with terror. It was not the usual venue he found himself in. Mott Haven was the sort of place you'd go to if you had a death wish, and certainly not the neighborhood you'd hang out in at any time of the day, much less at ten o'clock at night. William knew the risks but had called the meeting, nonetheless.

In the distance, gunshots and police sirens echoed in the night air, accompanied by the ceaseless barking of what seemed like every hound in the city. As William waited, alone in the shadowy corner, his senses were in overdrive. He had taken the train from Fifth Avenue and switched lines twice to get there—a terrifying experience in itself. He dreaded walking the mere five minutes from Mott Haven subway to the parking garage. But he'd taken what he deemed sufficient precautionary measures by dressing down in black slouchy pants and a matching black hoodie that he'd hoped would cover his strawberry blond hair and help him blend in. To minimize the risk of inviting an assault, he also left his Rolex and mobile phone behind, instead, carrying a snub-nosed revolver he had bought through one of the bouncers at a nightclub he frequently visited. A purchase the bouncer understood was, considering his father's recent murder, for protection and therefore didn't query the transaction.

From the shadows in the far corner, a sudden noise had a fresh supply of adrenaline shoot through William's veins. His fingers tightened around the firearm he had hidden in the kangaroo pocket of his hoodie, flinching as the hard steel pushed back into his bones and forced him to release his grip. He kept his eyes pinned on the spot the noise had come from, forced to blink several times to adjust his eyes to the dark. He knew he had left enough travel time to get there early, but in that moment he queried if perhaps his decision was foolish and that he'd inadvertently opened himself up to being a target of roaming gangs.

Footsteps drew closer, possibly two pairs, but it could have been more. He quick-blinked his eyes and cocked his head until he could distinguish two dark figures moving toward him. He thought of drawing his gun, then second-guessed it, deciding he'd wait it out a bit longer. If it was his guy, the gun would send the wrong signals and threaten everything he'd hoped to accomplish with this meeting. As he watched them draw closer, a fresh fear came to mind. He had never met them before. How would he know it was them? His heart pounded hard against his chest, his throat and mouth were bone dry. The men stopped roughly three yards away, then a small blue flame from a match moved to a cigarette in one man's mouth and illuminated both their faces. Of Indian descent, William instantly knew they were whom he had come there to meet.

He called out the man's name. A name he knew wasn't his actual one since it had once belonged to a well-known Indian healer he'd learned about during his studies, but it was what he'd been told to call him.

"Sushruta?"

Silence. Then, a high-pitched voice came back, "Dr. Sutton."

Again, silence.

William's heart skipped three beats.

"You missed a delivery," the man eventually said, dragging on his glowing cigarette.

"I know, sorry."

William took a step forward in an attempt to see the man's face more clearly, but the man took two steps back and lowered his head instead.

"You know the rules. It's a bad idea to break them."

"Of course, sorry."

He didn't know the rules but apologized anyway.

"Your father broke the rules."

It wasn't as much the meaning of the words that made William's skin crawl as it was the tone with which Sushruta said it; ominous, telling him to stay within the boundaries. To not do what his father did.

"Yes."

"I'm assuming you're taking over."

"That's actually why I wanted to meet."

"Well, we've met. Don't miss the next delivery. You'll get instructions."

"Yes, about that—" William started saying, but as quickly as Sushruta had appeared, he'd vanished into the shadows.

"No… wait!"

But the two men had already faded into the darkness.

William moved faster toward the dark void that seemed to have swallowed them. Hopeful that he could catch up with them, he rounded the corner and exited the parking garage. But he soon regretted his decision when instead, he was greeted by a group of five burly men who it seemed were out on the prowl for easy prey. Their aggressive demeanor told him they owned that part of the neighborhood, and it was very evident they spelled nothing but trouble. The kind of trouble William knew he'd never survive.

So he did what any entitled person who had lived under the protection of his family's wealth would do in a crime-riddled neighborhood on the south side of the Bronx. He ran. As fast as his legs would allow. But he was in unknown territory, and it didn't take the gang long to catch up with him. The next thing William knew he was face down on the sidewalk and on the receiving end of a multitude of punches and kicks to his body. As his mind zoned out to cope with the pain, he became vaguely aware of police sirens drawing closer. Moments later, as he struggled to gain his breath, his attackers scattered like birds being scared away by a cat. Next to his ear, he heard a male voice asking if he was okay. He wasn't, but he couldn't answer. The two police officers attempted to pull him to his feet, but as William slowly came to his senses, he held his head down and hoped they wouldn't see his face.

"Are you okay?" one asked.

"I'm fine. It's nothing."

"You don't look fine. We should take you to get checked out."

William's breath caught in his throat.

"No... thanks, I'm fine."

The police officer's eyes narrowed with suspicion as William straightened and his skin color came into view.

"You don't look like you belong in this neighborhood, sir. Care to tell us what you were doing here so late at night?"

William wiped the blood that had pooled in the corner of his mouth on the back of his sleeve. If they identified him, he'd have no way of explaining why he was there. Detective Kane already suspected him.

"I accidentally took the wrong train and got lost. I was making my way back to the subway when they attacked me."

The police officer's stern eyes told him he didn't believe him. But William knew they had no reason to take him in for questioning, so would have to let him go. He just needed to remain calm.

"Well, the subway is that way," the police officer continued.

"Oh, right, like I said, I got lost."

The two officers still weren't convinced, but when an urgent call sounded over their radio William knew he was off the hook.

"I'm fine, really." William exploited the welcome opportunity.

"Take a right over there and keep straight. The subway's a bit further down on your left."

"Thank you, officer."

"And stay away from the dark alleys," one shouted as his partner responded to the call.

William raised one hand to thank them and quickly

set off towards the subway. Feeling vulnerable, his hand instinctively reached for the safety of his gun.

But his gun was no longer there.

He stopped, stuck his hand deeper inside the pocket, patted his body down, but there was nothing there. Panic rushed through his bruised body as William realized the gun must have fallen out during the scuffle. He glanced back in the direction he'd come from, scanning the surrounding pavement, but it was gone. To his right, his eyes caught sight of a new group of men lurking in the shadows of a dark alley on the opposite side of the street. He'd be dead if he stuck around or went back to look, so he picked up his pace and continued on to the subway. Keeping his head hidden beneath his hood and his head looking down at his feet, he increased his gait. Conscious of a vehicle approaching from behind, its music blasting louder than the engine's noise, he looked up for the first time. The subway was less than thirty yards away. He had two options: play it cool or run. He chose the latter with no contemplation. The car increased in speed and drove in tandem with his pace. They shouted at him, asked him if he wanted a good time, then laughed. It was clear they were pimps, the thought of which repulsed William. Relief settled in the moment his feet hit the first steps of the subway and he leaped down the stairs three steps at a time. With the disco car's ridicule fading into the distance, he made his way to the platform and disappeared into the safety of the train that had already prepared to make its departure.

With one arm clutching his ribcage, he sank into one of the seats, grateful for his three narrow escapes. The night hadn't gone how he had planned; a predicament that left him gasping for air. Sushruta had been very clear, he wasn't to miss the next delivery or he'd end up dead just like his father.

And without his father's logbook, there was little he could do to save the situation. Either way, he was doomed.

In the window next to him, his reflection was no longer that of an entitled rich kid passing his days at the country club. Instead, the etched lines in his face and purple patches on his jaw resembled a man cornered. Like a deer trapped in a hunter's snare.

For the first time in his life, William knew the pressures of his legacy. Suddenly everything he'd thought he once wanted in life no longer mattered. All that mattered was to correct his wrongs. Anger welled up inside him. He watched his eyes turn near black, his knuckles white as he clenched his fists together. If his father wasn't already dead, he'd have killed him with his bare hands for landing him with this. He'd never asked to be born into his father's empire, never wanted it. All he had ever wanted was a simple life. His own life. But even that his father had taken with him to his grave. His life was never his to begin with and, even from beyond his grave, his father's grip on it remained.

The image in the mirror scared him, and he shut his eyes. He thought of his mother, incapacitated, waiting to let out her last breath. She deserved more. He owed it to her to see this thing through.

Even if it killed him.

CHAPTER TWELVE

A dam paced the coffee shop as his mind tried to make sense of what he'd just seen. The fresh coffee he'd bought had already gone cold in his hand, and he hadn't had so much as a single sip. His fingers rapped rhythmically against the paper cup in his hand. Its purpose no longer the caffeine boost he so desperately needed but instead an object that now helped him stay focused. There was no mistaking it. The man they'd rescued and cared for was wanted for murder. The situation had him doubt his judgment. He had seen this man's eyes, decided to trust him. His mind told him it was a mistake. His heart told him the opposite. For reasons unknown to him, he sensed he'd been placed in the young man's path to help, to protect him. Conflicted, the quiet conversation in his head turned to prayer. He asked God to reveal the truth, to help him trust God's judgment instead of his own. He prayed God would protect them, deliver them from all evil.

A few steps to his right, he placed the cup on the counter and apologized to the barista for not drinking it.

"Sorry, it got cold."

"I can make you a fresh cup if you'd like," the young girl offered, her smile as wide as the Grand Canyon.

He turned it down and prepared to walk away, then stopped when his eye caught the pile of newspapers at the end of the counter. He picked one up, noting the date to be current, and reached for some change in his pocket.

"You can take one, sir, they're free." The barista smiled.

Adam thanked her and popped a few coins in her tips jar, which made her smile widen even more.

At a nearby table, he spread the daily newspaper open, his eyes searching the headlines as fast as his fingers flipped the pages. And there it was, in big bold letters with a photo of the victim's bloodied corpse sprawled on the floor, and next to it, a headshot photo of Jonah. The article made mention of his name, Patrick Phillips. The victim was Dr. William (Bill) Sutton Senior, founder and owner of Gencorp Holdings, America's largest healthcare network and a prominent member of the medical community. Law enforcement had reason to believe that Phillips was somehow involved as he'd gone missing the night of the incident, and was calling on anyone who might know his whereabouts to come forward.

Adam's eyes took in the rest of the article while his stomach knotted up with each sentence he read. He thought of making a call to the Wilmington police, but something held him back.

He decided he'd sit on the information for now. Just until he knew the results of the tests—and until he knew what God wanted him to do. So, he twice folded the newspaper in half and zipped it up inside his jacket. Once he got back to The Lighthouse, he'd discuss it with Jim and Daniel. They'd know what to do.

Almost as soon as Adam had found his way back to the waiting room where he'd barely sat down, Jonah's doctor came to meet him.

"Pastor Cross?" he called out.

Adam jumped to his feet, "Yes, that's me. Please call me Adam."

The doctor agreed with a smile.

"I'm Dr. Brady. We have the results of the tests. The CT scan showed a subdural hematoma as a result of his head injury. Temporary memory loss is one of the symptoms, as is the confusion you described. Everything else looks to be fine, but there's a serious risk of blood clots, so we had no other option than to sedate him for the time being. He'll need to stay for a few days at the very least until we're certain he's out of danger."

"I don't understand. He seemed fine."

"So it appears, but a few more hours and he'd have been in real trouble. These conditions rarely display external symptoms. Just moving around increases his risk of an aneurysm. He's lucky to have come in when he did."

The doctor's demeanor showed his discomfort about what he was going to say next.

"I have to ask how well you know this man, Adam?"

Adam knew what was coming.

"Not well, actually not at all. He washed up on our beach and we rescued him from the storm, that's it."

The doctor's thin lips pressed together as if he was trying to keep his mouth from saying something he shouldn't but then he continued.

"We're finding ourselves in a rather uncomfortable situation. It appears he might have been involved in an incident upstate. The police are on their way. I had no choice, I'm legally bound to report his whereabouts to the authorities. I'm sorry."

"I understand, Doctor. I just read the news report in the coffee shop downstairs. What's going to happen to him?"

"For now, nothing. He'll remain sedated and in our care until we feel he's out of danger from blood clots or any other complications. The police will want to question him once he wakes up, provided his memory returns. You should go home, there's nothing we can do now but wait."

"How long does it take for the swelling to go down?"

"No idea. It can be a few days or a few weeks. It all depends on how quickly his body heals. If the pressure doesn't release on its own, we'll have to operate, but it's too soon to say." He looked over his shoulder, then whispered, "I'm not supposed to do this, but given that you are a man of faith and clearly concerned for his wellbeing, I'll let you know when his condition improves or if anything changes."

"Thank you, Doctor, I appreciate that. I know I shouldn't but I somehow feel responsible for him. He doesn't have any idea what's going on. He can't even remember his name. I wouldn't be doing my job if I didn't stand in the gap for him."

"I understand, Adam. You have my word, I'll keep you posted." Doctor Brady smiled, shook his hand, then left.

As with all small coastal towns where any noteworthy information travels faster than lightning, the town had already caught wind of the alleged murderer who'd washed up on their shore by the time Adam's taxi rolled into Turtle Cove. As it happens, Roxane Dixon, the town's gossip queen, was the first to *accidentally* run into him the moment he stepped out on the sidewalk a short way down the road from her internet café. In hindsight, Adam should've seen it coming, but he had hoped the news hadn't reached her ears yet—a wish upon a dream since Roxane knew just about everyone with a loose tongue within a fifty-mile radius.

"Yoo-hoo, Pastor Adam!" she flagged him down and caught up to him far too quickly. "Is it true you rescued the guy who murdered that rich man from New York? Tell me it isn't true!"

"Hey, Roxane, how are you?" He tried to derail her, but she wouldn't have it. When Roxane Dixon latched onto a story, she never let go.

"Is it true, Pastor? Lesley from the library says her daughter's new boyfriend told her. He's a doctor at the Wilmington Hospital, you know, and she says he saw the police with his own eyes. And this man spent the night at The Lighthouse? He could've murdered all of y'all in your sleep!" She held one flat hand on her hefty bosom while her big eyes searched his face for the details.

"Now, now, best we don't jump to any conclusions, Roxane. We don't know anything for certain."

"But it was him, wasn't it?"

"We're not sure. He has a head injury that's caused temporary memory loss, so until he regains his memory, no one knows what happened. And we shouldn't be judging anyone before we've heard his side of the story."

Adam attempted to excuse himself, but her plump body was as quick as her assumptions.

"I looked it up, you know, his admission sheet," her voice turned to a whisper. "Actually, Oliver *accidentally* found his way into the hospital's database, but there wasn't a photo attached. He's a smart one, that boy of mine, but don't tell anyone," she said, knowing full well Adam wouldn't repeat it.

"Ah, now I didn't need to know that, Roxane. You shouldn't have told me, and you should know better than to allow your son to break the law."

"Sorry, Pastor, it's just that, well, you've obviously seen the killer's face, so if there's one person in this town that can verify if he is the one in their file, then it's you. You owe it to our community to keep us safe, Pastor." She cleverly played her trump card.

The look in his eyes told her what she needed to know. Her sneaky hint of his pastoral duty to the community had paid off. She hooked her arm around his elbow and nudged him toward her shop.

"What if he is guilty, huh, Pastor? Have you thought of that?"

He had, but he didn't tell her he'd already battled the issue out with his conscience. And there was something else in his mind he tried hard to conceal.

"There it is!" she exclaimed, pushing her porky index finger towards his face.

"What is?"

"That look, I know that look. It's the same look you had that day you came home from school when that annoying Robbie boy lay into that poor new kid. What was his name? Ah yes, Darren something or other. You had caught the whole thing on the beta cam you carried everywhere with you. You have something, don't you?"

He ignored her, tried looking away. But she was onto him.

"Actually, Roxane, would you mind if I use one of your computers, please? Our power's still out at the mission and I'm probably now stuck here till morning."

"Only if you tell me what you have," she took a chance to which Adam replied, "Come now, Roxane, certain things need to remain within the church."

It was all he could say to avoid lying, but the look on Roxane Dixon's face told him she'd already read the truth behind his attempt to throw her off the scent.

"All right then, come along, but whatever you're hiding, you promise me you'll tell me first, okay?"

Less than a minute later, she had Adam settled in at one of her computers and instructed her son to take care of him while she quickly popped out—no doubt to pass on what her amateur detective skills had gained.

Relieved over her leaving, Adam's fingers hit the keyboard in search of any information the internet held on Patrick Phillips. A few newspapers had already printed several stories about his background, but other than that, there was nothing about the case. Disappointed, he sat back in his chair, then reached for the notebook he'd found in Patrick's clothes. But no matter how hard he stared at the writing on the pages, it still meant nothing to him.

His tummy growled, reminding him he hadn't eaten anything since Daniel's stack sandwich. It was late, and he was tired, but with the bridge still down, and the firehouse still dealing with the aftermath of the storm, he'd have to spend the night at Sue-Ellen's B&B.

With his eyes still glued to the leather journal in his hand, he walked over to the counter to settle his dues with Oliver. The youth must have been between games on his computer because, unlike his usual absentminded manner, Oliver immediately noticed the contents of the notebook.

"Hey, Pastor, I didn't know you were into pigeons."

CHAPTER THIRTEEN

Adam's face must have told Oliver something entirely different from what he felt inside.

"Sorry, Pastor Adam, I shouldn't have. I'm beginning to think I'm just like my mother, always poking where there shouldn't be any poking. Forget I said anything. It's none of my beeswax."

"No… it's fine… I… what are you talking about?" Adam eventually got out.

"Your pigeons."

Oliver pushed his chin out toward the notebook, surprised that Adam still didn't respond.

"Like I said, Pastor, I'm sorry. I didn't mean to—"

"Oliver, stop. What are you talking about, man?"

"Your notebook, it's got hundreds of pigeon numbers in. You know, the numbers on their rings, around their feet." His voice lifted into a question when he saw Adam still hadn't made sense of it all.

Adam stared at the writing for a brief second before Oliver's hand flattened the leather journal onto the counter between them. Bending his neck to one side to get a better angle, he pointed to the numbers with his index finger as he explained.

"Yup, these are pigeon numbers." He paused, then added, "Huh, how about that?"

"What?"

"Well, it's just that I would've expected they'd all be from around here, or at least just the States, but you've got quite a selection there."

"Okay," Adam said, confused.

"Are you racing internationally?"

Adam didn't answer. His mind was too busy trying to piece it all together.

"There I go again, sorry. It's really none of my business," Oliver apologized again.

"How do you know? That they're from all over the world."

"This here," Oliver pointed out two letters that repeated themselves every few pages, his fingers bouncing all over the pages.

"What do they mean?"

"These are the country codes, where they're from. Usually, they put the local racing federation's initials on them, but these are definitely country codes. See, US,

IN, NI, which I'm guessing is Nigeria. I know because we sometimes have to build these into our coding."

Adam scratched his head as if he didn't believe him.

"You can ask my professor, that's how I know all this. He's won all sorts of championships and stuff. He's obsessed with them. Prof. Thorpe's the coolest professor I've ever had. He's always finding ways to bring his pigeons into our lectures. Why I wouldn't know; it has nothing to do with computer sciences, but we let him tell us about them anyway. It breaks the boredom between creating *algos*. But you don't have to take my word for it, Pastor."

"No, it's not that. I believe you. It's just, well, I don't understand why he'd have a book with pigeon numbers in them."

"Who?"

Adam realized he'd better not say more for fear of Roxane spreading it all over town. He'd bet his last dollar she'd be interrogating her son the moment she set foot inside her shop again.

"Oh, nothing. Thanks for your help, Oliver. You stay safe now, okay?"

He buried the logbook in his pocket and dashed out the door before Roxane had a chance to return and corner him.

But Adam had barely got to the end of the block when he swung around and ran back to the shop, startling Oliver as he burst through the door.

"Sorry, Oliver, I just… " He struggled to find the words, then said awkwardly, "I'd love to meet your professor. He sounds like a fascinating man."

His declaration surprised Oliver, who took a few moments to process the situation.

"Oh, yeah, totally, he's awesome. Here, I guess he'd be fine with you calling him yourself. I mean, the guy loves talking about his birds and stuff so I don't see why not."

His thumb glided across his cellphone before he scribbled his professor's number on a piece of paper and handed it to Adam.

"Great, thanks, Oliver. Fascinating stuff," he added, sounding even more fake than before.

"Yeah, sure, Pastor. Good luck."

BY THE TIME ADAM SHUT THE DOOR TO ONE OF SUE-Ellen's rooms at her B&B, his heart was drumming hard in the pit of his stomach. Most of her rooms had gotten booked by townsfolk whose homes had flooded, and it took him a fair amount of time to escape the passing conversations before he could flee into the solitude of his room. He flung his jacket over the foot of his bed, then squeezed into the chair at the small bistro table, not bothering with pulling it away first. His fingers glided along each number sequence as if reading Braille, picking out the country codes as he went along. Several pages into the notebook, he'd already latched onto a pattern that had by now become too blatant to pass off as a coincidence. If Oliver were correct, and these were pigeons, he now saw a definite route unfold before his very eyes.

And the destination country was always the same.

India... US.

Nigeria... US.

Brazil... US.

Mexico... US.

Canada... US.

Then it started again. Same sequence, same countries.

When Adam's breathing became so rapid that he nearly hyperventilated he knew he was onto something. Something Phillip felt he needed to protect at all cost.

His eyes moved to the numbers that followed the country codes. The first few digits almost looked familiar, but he couldn't be certain. The rest made no sense to him at all. If he were to unlock the secret behind this journal, he'd have to find out what the numbers meant.

From his pocket, he grabbed the piece of paper on which Oliver had jotted down the professor's phone number. He reached across the bed and pulled the room telephone onto the bed. With shaky fingers, he dialed Professor Thorpe's phone number.

It rang.

He waited.

No answer.

He rang again. This time, a man answered.

"Hello."

"Is this Professor Thorpe?"

"It is, who's calling?"

"My name's Adam, I know one of your students, Oliver Dixon. He gave me your number."

"Ah yes, Mr. Dixon. He's a bright young man. How can I help you?"

"I need some information, about pigeons. He said you'd know."

The professor's voice changed, suddenly filled with joy.

"They're the most incredible creatures, aren't they? Super intelligent. You know, they choose you, not the other way around. And if you do it right, they'll be loyal to you till death."

Adam listened as the professor volunteered information, which, if given half the opportunity, he soon determined, would continue for hours.

"I didn't know that. Actually, I was hoping you could help me understand the numbers on their rings? What do they mean?"

"Why, have you found a lost one? They do sometimes get lost, not often, but it happens."

"No, no, I haven't. I'm just doing some research, for a project." Adam bit down on his lip.

"Oh well, in that case, where do I even start? I can spend hours—"

"Perhaps another day, Professor, I'm a bit short on time, sorry," Adam added.

"That's quite alright. Life is busy and all."

The joy in the professor's voice had been replaced by disappointment, possibly even loneliness, and Adam instantly regretted cutting him short. He made a mental note to make it up to him somehow when all this was over.

There was a brief silence before he spoke again, his tone now more businesslike.

"The rings carry details about their ownership. You'll find the initials of the club they're registered with, then their hatch year, and finally their identity number. Each bird gets its own unique number, like a social security number. It tracks back to their owners."

"Really, so I'm able to find out who owns a particular bird."

"Exactly."

"How would I do this, Professor?"

"Oh, these days it's too easy. You just key it into a search engine and it'll pop right up. Unless it's a spy pigeon, of course," he bellowed a laugh.

It was clearly a joke, but the words piqued Adam's interest.

"You get spy pigeons?"

"For sure!" The passion in his voice was back.

"They've been around for three thousand years. That's how the Roman and Greek soldiers communicated with their armies during wars. Of course, it has evolved quite a bit since then. The Germans even went as far as inventing a tiny spy camera that attached to their chests, taking imagery of enemy camps and everything. It was genius! I mean, who'd suspect a pigeon, right? They can fly miles and miles across enemy lines, delivering coded messages, and no one would ever know it. A drone, you notice, but a pigeon, it's just another bird in the sky. And the stealth with which they escaped bullets and bombs, let me tell you, to this day nothing compares."

He cleared his throat, stopping himself from waffling on too much.

"That's remarkable. You said they fly miles and miles. Can they fly between countries?"

"That depended on the distance. Some pigeons can fly over a thousand miles, but it's not too common. What they'd do instead is take them closer to their destination by car, train, even a boat. Then they'd have them fly the rest of the distance to deliver the message, usually about fifty miles or so. But here's the thing, while they could be released from anywhere in the world, they'd only ever arrive at one location—their home roost."

Adam was on his feet, pacing his tiny room as he processed the information.

"Hang on, Professor. You're saying, that if a pigeon

has to deliver a message, let's say between India and the United States, hypothetically speaking, of course, it will be released somewhere within fifty miles of its home, in either direction."

"Astounding, isn't it? They survive even the toughest circumstances."

"They sure are, Professor. I can't thank you enough for helping me, thank you."

"You're most welcome. Perhaps when your project is done and dusted, you'd like to see them first-hand. Just give me a ring."

Adam ended the call and stared at the numbers in the notebook. It had all become vividly clear to him now. For reasons still unknown to him, Patrick had recorded the identification numbers of hundreds of pigeons most likely used to deliver secret messages between these countries. Countries that would generally be considered insignificant and non-threatening against the US, or any other country for that matter. He might have expected secret communications involving Russia or China, but why India, why Nigeria? They were hardly capable of initiating any kind of attack.

And while Adam had a hard time wrapping his mind around all he had just learned, he knew one thing for certain. Patrick Phillips might not be as innocent as he had hoped.

CHAPTER FOURTEEN

W illiam rushed to shut the door to his father's office the moment he recognized the number on his mobile. He had taken over the executive office at Gencorp HQ, and he was acutely aware of Lydia's attention to his every move. She had been his father's assistant for nearly thirty years, and her loyalty to Bill Sutton ran deep—even beyond his death.

"You'd better be calling me with good news, Mikey," he said as he sat down behind the oversized antique desk that still looked as if Bill had been there moments ago.

"That depends," the caller replied.

"Don't play games with me, Mikey. We've known each other a long time, but I don't have the time nor the patience for silly games." Mikey had been head of security for Gencorp for nearly a decade. "Did you track down your guy or not?"

"Yes."

"Well, did he find the book?"

"No, not yet, but he knows where it is."

"Go on, man, spit it out."

"You're not going to like it, Wills."

William didn't respond.

"Remember, he said he'd walked in on the killer hiding in your father's study."

"Yes, yes, he had the journal and your guy was too sloppy and he got away." William rolled his hand in the air for Mikey to hurry the story along as if he could see it.

Mikey cleared his throat.

"He knows who the guy is, and where to find him."

"You said that already. I think we already know who was responsible for killing my father. I'm not interested in the killer, just the book, Mikey!"

"It was Patrick, Wills. Patrick has the book. My guy recognized his picture in the papers."

William was on his feet, staring at the floor in front of him.

"Patrick? That's impossible. Why would he take the notebook? He has nothing to do with this. It doesn't make any sense."

"Unless he killed your father, Wills."

"No way, not Patrick, your guy's wrong."

"Nope, he's dead certain. Have you considered that he could be working for them?"

"Phillips? Not a chance. That's the most ridiculous thing I've heard all week. He's too much of a goody-two-shoes to be in bed with these guys. No way."

"Money has a way of turning your closest friends into your biggest enemies, Wills. The root of all evil and all that stuff."

"Yeah, not Patrick, he's not like that. I've known him all my life, you know that. He's like a brother to me, and money's never been what makes him tick."

"The guy's a Wall Street trader, William. He strategizes wealth all day long. Of course, money's what makes him tick. What else could it be, huh? Why else would he have been there? He killed your father and took the notebook. Think about it."

Mikey let the thought sit with William before he spoke again.

"Either way, he has it and we now know where he is. My guy knows someone on the inside, a cop. Apparently, the storm dragged Patrick all the way down the coast. He's in a hospital, in Wilmington. Say the word and I can have my guy there by morning. The place is crawling with police, but he'll find a way in."

William lifted the phone away from his ear and put the back of his phone hand to his mouth. He was fully aware what Mikey's *guy* was capable of and that he had a reputation for getting what he wanted no matter the consequences. That's why Mikey kept him in his back pocket—for occasions just like this one. But that could potentially mean he'd go as far as killing Patrick if he needed to.

A lump formed in William's throat. How had it come to this? As an only child, he'd always seen Patrick as the brother he never had. They had been friends since before they could ride a bike.

"Wills, you still there?" Mikey's voice rang out into the silence.

"Yeah, I'm here."

"Just say the word."

There was silence, then William spoke.

"I don't want more blood on my hands, got it? He's not to touch Patrick, is that clear, Mikey? Not a single hair on his body!"

"Copy that."

The line went dead.

William dropped his cell on his desk and stared at an empty spot on the wall. His mind lingered on the information. The thought of Patrick killing his father made him sick. They had had their differences, that he knew, but he'd never thought he'd go as far as killing him. Would he?

As William's mind searched for a motive, he recalled a conversation his father had had with him over lunch just a few short weeks ago. It was one of the few business lunches he had ever had with his father and it was to inform him he was going to fire Patrick, that he'd lost the company millions, and that the only reason he'd tolerated him that long was because he was William's best friend. They had gotten into an argument over it and he had walked out on his father. He had defended Patrick, vouched for him, begged his father to reconsider and give him another chance.

Was it possible his father had ignored his pleas and fired him at the charity dinner the other night? Patrick could've gotten angry, retaliated, and killed him.

Or he could be the traitor Mikey said he was and working with Sushruta.

William stood up and stared out the window.

Patrick had every reason to kill his father. Investo wouldn't exist without Gencorp Holdings. And Patrick knew William would never fire him once he took over from his father.

William's insides felt as if someone had punched him. Then anger set in. Patrick had played him, taken him for a fool. He was a murderer, a traitor, working for the other side. After all these years, the man he thought he knew was a stranger, a cold-blooded killer.

Blinded by his anger, he scooped up his cell and dialed Mikey's number.

"Yes?"

"Do whatever you have to, Mikey, I don't care. Just get me that logbook."

He ended the call without exchanging another word, then stormed out of the office.

DETECTIVE KANE DROPPED THE RECEIVER BACK INTO place and stared at the open folder on his desk.

"Who was that?" Jones asked.

"Wilmington police, they found him."

"Phillips? What's he doing there?"

"He was brought in after his yacht ran ashore in a small town somewhere along the coast. Turtle Cove, or something. Can you believe it?"

"And he's alive?"

"Yep, he actually survived a hurricane at sea."

Jones let out a whistle to convey her awe and watched as Kane walked into the chief's office to report the news. Barely a minute later, he was back.

"The chief wants us on the next flight out, even though the guy's still sedated. He's having Lucy make the arrangements as we speak."

"We're going to Wilmington now... at almost nine o'clock at night?"

"You have something better to do tonight?"

"I guess not." She threw her hands up and leaned back in her chair.

Kane tapped the back of his pencil on the papers in front of him.

"Do you believe in God?"

His question caught her off guard.

"Wowzer, partner, what's gotten into you? In our five years together on the squad, staring at each other across these desks every day, you've never even come close to asking me that. You okay?"

Kane walked to the nearby coffee station and refilled his mug, then sat halfway on the edge of her desk.

"I guess I'm just curious, you know."

"No, I don't know."

"Think about it. A man like Bill Sutton, a highly respected philanthropist who's done nothing but good work in his life, gets murdered by a guy who's the exact opposite, yet he survives a massive hurricane. Where's the fairness in that?"

Jones pondered her police partner's musings, then, as she too got up to pour a fresh cup of coffee, said, "Well, life isn't fair, Kane. But all I know is that there has to be a higher power who decides life and death. How he decides whose number to call and when, I can't answer, but this stuff is all my brother talked about after he came back from Iraq. When he died, I had the same questions you're asking right now. I mean, he serves fifteen months surviving one of the worst wars ever and comes home unscathed, only to be hit by a stray bullet in a local gang fight. How does that make sense? His biggest crime in life was choosing to convert from Catholicism to Protestantism. He believed in God, went to church every Sunday, and yet he got killed. All

129

because he was in the wrong place at the wrong time. He did good things too, all the time. I guess if it's your time then it's your time."

Kane slipped off Jones' desk and gulped two large mouthfuls of his coffee before placing the rest back on his desk. Grabbing his blazer from the back of his chair, he said, "Yeah, well, I might not have control over who dies, but I can control catching these criminals and not letting them get away with it. I say we push Phillips for a confession the moment he wakes up, and then we throw away the key."

"You still think a guy like Phillips would kill a man who was practically his father. What happened to innocent until proven guilty?"

"Oh, he's guilty all right. We have proof."

"Proof! What, his cellphone outside Bill Sutton's office? That's not enough to convict, and you know it. There wasn't one fingerprint inside the office, no surveillance showing him walking in or out of the office, nothing. It's circumstantial at best."

They turned and walked toward the elevator when Jones spoke again. "You know, Kane, have you ever thought that perhaps Bill Sutton had more enemies? Everyone has enemies. I can't believe that he was such a saint that he only ever had one, much less it being a guy whose sole job it is to make him more money. I can't wrap my head around that. Just because he did good works by giving away his money to every charity out there doesn't mean everyone liked him. People like Bill Sutton don't go around never upsetting anyone."

They entered the lift when the doors opened.

"Right now, Jonesy, all evidence points to Phillips, so unless there's something that persuades me to believe otherwise, I'm going to follow where it leads me. I'll get the truth out of him the moment he opens his eyes."

CHAPTER FIFTEEN

I t was just after seven a.m. when Adam arrived back at The Lighthouse. He had caught a ride with the Coast Guard since they needed to investigate the yacht, which still lay wedged between the rocks in the cove. Adam hadn't slept all night. Haunted by the news that Patrick had not only killed a man but was in all probability also involved with dangerous activities, had left him tossing and turning all night.

While he strolled from the cove up toward the mission, his mind still worked through his anguish. Had he never met the man, he'd have been fine with everything, but he *had* met him. He'd looked into his eyes, seen deep into his soul, sensed he was a good man, certain he'd felt God's assurance. How then was it that he was so wrong to trust the situation?

But as soon as the doubtful thought crossed his

mind, the Holy Spirit snatched it right back and reminded him he should, and *could* trust God. That though in the physical realm all pointed to a man undeserving of his trust, the spiritual realm declared the contrary. And since his flesh lived in the physical while his spirit lived in a heavenly realm that transcended all understanding, he was set apart from those who believed with the eyes of their heads instead of with the eyes of their hearts. Reminded of the proverb that said he was to not lean on his own understanding, he'd have to let go of all that made sense on earth and not waiver from trusting God.

Peace enveloped his heart and settled in the corners of his soul. His heart knew what it knew, and that was all he needed.

WITH HEART AND MIND IN HARMONY, ADAM FOUND Daniel and Jim in the church. They were each standing on ladders, busy covering the broken window with a sheet of plexiglass—which was nothing but an outdated signage poster that Jim had dug out of the storeroom.

"I'm thinking we should keep it up permanently," Adam said as he entered.

"Hey, when did you get back? How's Jonah?" an enthused Daniel asked the moment he saw him.

"I just arrived. How are you guys? Need some help?"

Adam disappeared between a set of pews to pick up a hymn book that had fallen to the floor underneath it before joining them under the window.

"Just finishing off here, thanks," Jim answered then continued, "Is Jonah okay?"

"I'm going to say yes even though there's a… let's call it a complication."

The two men were already halfway down their ladders when he continued.

"You might want to sit down for this."

"Nothing serious, is it?" Daniel asked, taking a seat in a nearby pew.

"His name's not Jonah, it's Patrick Phillips. And he's wanted for murder."

"Murder! What are you talking about, Adam?" Daniel's voice was loaded with disbelief as he said it.

"I know. It pains me to say it, but it's true. Here, look." Adam pulled the folded newspaper from inside his jacket.

The stunned expressions on their faces told him that they too were having the same doubts he'd been set free from just a short while ago.

Daniel rubbed a flat hand across his face as if to wake himself up from a nightmare.

"There's more though," Adam started again, pausing a few seconds for their emotions to settle down.

"I suspect he's an informant of sorts." He pulled out the notebook.

"You mean like a spy? For who?" Jim asked.

"Not sure, and yes, it sounds crazy, I know, and it doesn't make any sense whatsoever, but this here," he pointed to the number sequences in the notebook, "these are pigeon identification numbers."

"Pigeons! What?" Daniel scoffed beneath a surprised expression. "That's the most ridiculous thing I've ever heard, son. These could mean anything," he added.

"I know, it sounds ridiculous, but I've had it verified. They're also not just any pigeons, Daniel. They are carrier pigeons, like the ones who fly hundreds of miles to deliver a message before they find their way back to their homes."

"I've read about these," Jim said. "They're amazing."

Adam nodded. "So I hear, and these ones fly everywhere. Nigeria, Brazil, Canada, Mexico, even India. Patrick kept a record of it, logged hundreds of birds. All in a particular sequence."

"What on earth for? And who told you he was a spy?" Daniel said, sounding almost defensive.

"No one, but it's rather obvious, isn't it? We find him with nothing of value other than this book, only to find out he had killed one of the most influential businessmen upstate just days before he washed up on our beach."

"Still doesn't make him a spy."

"You're right, but there's a chance that he is. From what I understand, these pigeons are dropped off fifty or so miles from their target address, which in this case is between two countries, or at least a home coop of sorts. They'd fly from this drop-off point to the destination where they deliver the message. The recipient then sends a message back with the same pigeon to the same original drop-off location, their roost. Patrick was on a boat. According to my expert, this is the most likely transport method they use. It's quite genius."

"Have you asked him?" Jim said.

"I can't, at least not yet. His head injury posed a risk of blood clots, so they're having to sedate him until the swelling subsides. He's still at the hospital but the police have him under watch."

"I've met a lot of people in my life, Adam, and I can tell you right now. Patrick isn't a killer," Daniel said.

Adam smiled.

"I'm relieved to hear you say that, Daniel. I sensed the same. I couldn't sleep last night thinking I'd misjudged him, misunderstood what the Holy Spirit told me. But on the way here I prayed about it again, and I am very certain we're meant to help him. I believe it's what God wants us to do. This guy survived a hurricane at sea and out of all the places along this coast, he washed up right here on ours. I'd say that's a God-incidence."

"Jonah and the whale," Jim said. "God showed

Jonah mercy for a reason, so he could come to his senses and turn to God. We don't know what this young man's life is about and where he stands with God, but his life got spared. Right now everyone thinks he's guilty of murder and the last time I checked, you've been using your God-given talent to help catch the bad guys."

Daniel placed his hand on Adam's shoulder.

"I agree with Jim. I'm reminded of the scripture in Ephesians. *We are his workmanship, created in Christ Jesus for good works, which God prepared beforehand, that we should walk in them.* I'd say your good works are needed here, Adam, physically and spiritually. So how about you go catch the real killer and see where God takes it?"

The more Jim and Daniel spoke, the harder it was for Adam to contain the thrilling sensation that now flooded his insides and threatened to erupt without warning. Their words had confirmed what he'd already sensed God wanted him to do, and it pushed him to his feet.

"I need to get back to the hospital, I need to speak to Patrick before they get to him *and* before they arrest him."

"There's only one problem," Jim said. "The bridge is still out. Won't be fixed for at least a week if we're lucky. We're stuck here."

"If I hurry, I might be able to catch a ride back again

with the Coast Guard and hitch a ride to Wilmington with one of the relief crew. I'll figure the rest out along the way."

Adam was already halfway to the door when he yelled for them to keep him and Patrick in their prayers. Inside his belly was a fire he knew could not be ignored. One he'd felt each time he helped Gabriel solve a case and missed each time it was over. He had sensed God was preparing him for something a few times before, but it hadn't become more clear than in that very moment.

When Adam finally managed to find his way back to the hospital in Wilmington, he hastily made his way towards Phillip's room. The elevator took forever, and he jabbed his finger at the call button in an attempt to hurry it along. But it made no difference. Unable to contain the pressing desire to speak to Patrick, he decided he'd take the stairs instead—his room was only two floors up. So he dashed around the corner and entered the stairwell. His feet ascended two steps at a time until halfway between floors, a doctor rushed past him, nearly knocking him off his feet. Their eyes only met for a brief second, but that was all it took to convey the chilling message that lay heavy in his eyes.

"Sorry!" Adam apologized in vain as he turned and watched the man disappear down the stairwell.

By the time Adam burst through the stairwell door to the second floor, he was ready to do what God had called him to. But as he neared Patrick's room, he noticed a flurry in the hallway outside the door. Nurses and doctors were running in and out of his room. Several police officers ran towards him while two stayed and stood guard on either side of the room, their bodies on high alert.

As he got closer, his excitement gradually faded to become a ball of knots that weighed his entire body down.

Confused, he ran to the nurses' station looking for answers.

"What happened, what's going on?"

One of the nurses recognized him and was quick to answer, her voice a low whisper. "Someone tried to kill Mr. Phillips. Dr. Brady walked in on him and nearly got killed fighting the guy off. If he hadn't decided to start his rounds earlier than usual this morning, your friend would've been dead."

"So he's okay?"

"They're still with him. He lost a lot of blood. The guy tried to make it look like a suicide. Slit both his wrists."

Adam took a few steps to one side as one of the nurses pushed past him. Inside, his emotions rushed like a torrential river while his mind tried to catch up with what had just happened. As a timeline slowly took shape in his mind, there was no denying that what he now suspected must have been the killer had nearly pushed him down the stairs. Loud footsteps rushed towards him from behind. He swung around to see a man and woman running towards the scene, each holding out a gold badge. The man's shoulder nudged his as he pushed past Adam into Patrick's room.

Adam found his body following as if it had a mind of its own.

"You can't go in there, sir," a police officer stopped him.

"I think I just passed the guy who did this," Adam said, his voice strangely lacking emotion.

The officer's eyes stretched open. "Where?" he urged as he readied his transmission radio.

"On the stairwell between the first and second floors. He was dressed in scrubs, wearing a surgical mask but no hat. He had dark hair and dark eyes."

CHAPTER SIXTEEN

In the moments that followed, the corridor outside Patrick's room was teeming with police officials and medical staff. Adam watched as the officers scattered in search of the man who had just tried to kill Patrick. From where he now stood in the doorway, he watched the harrowing scene around Patrick's bed play out. A nurse exchanged the clear IV bag for one filled with blood, while another finished dressing his wrists. Beneath the bed, there were large pools of blood on the floor and even more on the bedding. To one side, the man and woman who had rushed past him earlier stood talking to Dr. Brady while a nurse tended to a large cut across his cheek.

While Adam couldn't hear what they were saying, it was obvious from the notes the woman took down in a small black pocketbook that they were police detectives taking down Dr. Brady's statement.

And while none of them knew the reason behind the attempted murder, Adam did.

He knew, now more than ever before, that the leather journal held all the secrets, and that someone else was after it.

It would be so easy to hand the notebook over to the detectives and tell them what he knew. He'd be free to go back to the safety of The Lighthouse and carry on with his life, let them do what they were trained to do. Except he couldn't. Not only would that reinforce their suspicions that Patrick murdered the man from New York, but he'd also be failing in his duty. And although he knew full well he could never disappoint God because he was simply not powerful enough to derail God's plans, he would know deep down inside that he didn't trust God enough.

His eyes fell upon Patrick's face. His skin was pale and gray. Now lying between layers of clean bedding, he was peacefully unaware of what he'd be waking up to. With the police officers in pursuit of the killer and his way clear, Adam entered the room and walked the five paces to his bed. The nurses had all gone and, apart from Dr. Brady and the two detectives who were deep in conversation in the far corner of the room, he was alone at his bedside. Adam slipped his hand underneath Patrick's motionless fingers while he rested his other hand on his shoulder. In the silence of his mind, he prayed for Patrick and asked God to heal him, strengthen him, protect him. Then his prayers turned to asking God to guide his steps, help him. A few minutes of heavenward conversation was all Adam managed to steal before Dr. Brady's voice next to him brought him back into the present.

"He's going to be okay, Adam," he said gently.

Adam didn't reply. His ears had already tuned in to the detective's voice that spoke loudly into his cell behind him.

"Chief, you know the Feds will be all over this if we don't do something right now. We don't have a lot of time. They're foaming at the bit to get their hands on this case!"

"It's complicated, Adam," Dr. Brady spoke quietly when he saw what had grabbed Adam's attention. "They're pushing hard for a court order to move Patrick back to New York."

"Why?"

"I don't exactly know how these things work, but it has something to do with the FBI and NYPD losing jurisdiction if Patrick stays here. It's a high-profile case, and it's getting a lot of attention. They want him back in their state so they can get him to confess."

"And send him to jail for the rest of his life."

"Yes, looks that way."

"He didn't do it. Something else is going on here."

"They seem to disagree, Adam."

"There's got to be something you can do to prevent them from moving him. I need more time to figure this out."

"The court order will prevent me from sedating him. There's nothing I can do, Adam, and even if there was a way for me to keep him here, it wouldn't change anything. It would just be passed on to another police department. I'm sorry."

Adam suddenly felt as if the walls were closing in on him. He had come there to speak to Patrick, to ask him about the pigeons, the journal, and how he came to have it, but now that seemed impossible.

What do I do, Lord? Show me!

But the answers he so desperately needed didn't come.

"What I *can* do is delay it," Dr. Brady whispered. "There is a treatment protocol and a lot of paperwork involved in something like this."

Adam's heart skipped a beat.

"How long?"

"I'd say once the court order gets here, forty-eight hours at the most. I might be able to add a few more with signing off on the transfer, but that'd be pushing it. And if our servers accidentally go down, well, that's an entirely different situation then, isn't it?" His eyes twinkled as he said it.

"I'll take it, thanks, Doc."

Adam's mind was suddenly alive with prospects as he turned and left the room. With the doctor's help, he'd have two days at the most to get to the bottom of this. How he was going to do it, he didn't know, at least not yet.

Deep in thought, he didn't realize he had run the wrong way, and somehow he ended up at the other end of the hospital. Annoyed with himself for wasting time getting lost, he turned into the first elevator and hit the ground floor button with the back of his fist. Alone in the elevator, he leaned his head back against the mirrored wall behind him and waited for the numbered lights to count down to the ground floor.

"Please don't stop, please don't stop," he begged out loud when the elevator slowed down towards the first floor, only to find his begging ineffective. The doors opened onto a male nurse who stood waiting behind an elderly man in a wheelchair. The nurse was chatting to the man, flashing a row of perfectly straight teeth from behind a wide, friendly smile as they entered the lift.

Adam smiled back, even though on the inside, his emotions were running wild. He should've taken the stairs, he thought.

Next to him the nurse and his patient exchanged friendly banter about the advancement of technology and how things had changed so much over the years that nothing was private anymore, that it was out there for all who had the internet to see.

The words instantly shot through Adam's body like a bolt of lightning.

"Of course!" he exclaimed and threw both arms in the air as if he were cheering next to the football field.

His sudden reaction invited curious stares from his fellow elevator passengers.

"Sorry, I just had an idea come to me," he apologized with enthusiasm, then continued. "Say, you wouldn't by any chance know if there is a computer or internet station I could use, would you?"

"As it happens, yes, there is," the male nurse smiled. "When you get to the ground floor, turn right and continue down the corridor past the gift shop. You'll find a booth on your left. It sometimes needs a restart if it's been on idle for too long, and it's not the fastest, but hopefully, it will do the trick."

Adam leaned around them to jab the ground-level button again.

"It'll do, thank you, I just need to look up something real quick."

The doors finally parted and Adam forced his body through the narrow space not wanting to wait until the doors opened all the way.

"Thanks for sparking the idea, fellas," he yelled back and went in search of the computer, which he found easily at the precise spot where the nurse had said it would be. He'd been praying it didn't need a restart since he stepped out of the elevator.

The computer was built into a bright blue booth-like pod that resembled a cross between an arcade game and an ATM, with a touch-screen keyboard. Relieved it reacted to his fingertips the moment he pressed down on it, he mentally said a quick, *Thank you, Father.*

His fingers quickly moved over the screen as he typed a sentence into the internet search bar. A few more clicks and he found what he was after. He clicked the link and waited for the page to load. A quick glance over his shoulder confirmed that he was alone. Tucked away in his waistband under his shirt, he stole a sideways glance at one of the US pigeon numbers in the leather notebook and entered it into the online tracking tool. A few seconds later, the computer screen flashed the bird's physical details and a single address across the screen. Every ounce of energy inside his body was ready to explode with joy when he skimmed over the arbitrary street name before his eyes settled on the borough and state: Brooklyn, New York. Close enough that he could travel there. His stomach flipped upside down and inside out before it left his chest heaving with excitement. He reached for the pen dangling from a string on the nearby table and scribbled the address on his forearm before zipping back down the corridor towards the exit.

Less than an hour later, Adam had taken a taxi to the airport, bought his plane ticket, and was now settling into his seat on the flight to New York.

CHAPTER SEVENTEEN

Adam hadn't been to New York in a very long time, and he'd forgotten how lively it was. He'd also forgotten how challenging driving through the city traffic was. By the time the taxi dropped him off at the address he had taken down, it was almost three o'clock. In the afternoon sun, he stared at the building in front of him. It was a tall, narrow structure on the wrong side of town. The once white walls were almost black in several places from years of compacted dirt and there were several equally filthy windows spreading up over ten floors, a few of them broken with newspaper covering the holes. Where the windows were intact, he could just about make out the outlines of curtains. Doubts filled his mind over whether he'd copied the address correctly, even though he wasn't sure what he had expected to find. He checked the scribbled address that had already started to rub away. It matched.

The weathered front door opened, blasting a cacophony of noise and a small group of tattooed men out onto the steps in front of the building. From the way they were dressed and behaving, it was clear they weren't the most upstanding of characters, and Adam suddenly felt extremely vulnerable. It seemed they too had spotted him as they were now watching him from across the street. *Protect me, Lord!*

Adam broke eye contact, looked at his feet instead, and buried his hands in his pockets. Fear filled him as he realized what he'd encounter once he entered. A second later an equally shady car pulled up and, much to his relief, whisked the gold-chained gang away.

When Adam finally managed to get his heart rate back to normal, he found his feet stuck to the pavement. Unable to pluck up the courage to enter the building, he dropped his head back and filled his lungs with air. As he exhaled his anxiety, he spotted a flock of birds heading towards the building's roof. It took a few moments before he realized they were pigeons. He was at the right address, after all. He contemplated taking the fire escape to the roof but decided against it when he noticed the erosion on most of the ladders. He set off across the road and entered the building.

The noise inside was deafening. Loud music, women's screams, kids crying. There was no end to any of it. But he kept his head down and hurried along the dark corridor in search of the stairwell. When he finally found the even darker stairs, he wasn't sure if he'd pass out from fear or the putrid stench of urine that hit him square between the eyes. His feet leaped up three steps at a time and settled into a hurried rhythm. There were two occasions where he narrowly missed a few of the residents between floors as he made his way up to the roof. Out of breath and losing momentum, he passed two scantily clad women leaning against the wall to the entrance of the eighth-floor stairwell. He thought of greeting them but didn't. A decision he was glad he'd made when they promptly flirted with him and offered him promises of a good night. Their advances were what Adam needed to have him bolt the final few floors to the top, and he burst through the steel door onto the roof like a cork out of a champagne bottle. In desperate need of clean air—and all else that would relieve him from what he'd just gone through—he hunched over and leaned his hands on his knees.

From somewhere to his right, he heard the sound of birds flapping their wings and he turned his head towards the noise. His vision was obscured by a red brick outbuilding, but he could just about make out a few birds that were picking at something on the ground behind it. Taking precautions by using the structure as cover, he slowly moved toward them until he was in full view of about two dozen pigeons fighting over a patch of bird food. The nearby grumblings of a man's voice had Adam duck behind the building from where he now listened. The man was telling them not to fight, and that there was more than enough for everyone. He called a few out by name, scolding one with a warning before he scattered another fistful or two of birdseed.

The man, who sounded like a father breaking up a fight between his teenage sons, had stringy white hair sticking out from underneath a black newsboy hat that had seen better days. He wore a black melton jacket that was at least three sizes too big for him around his shoulders and dark green corduroy pants, which also seemed to drown his body. While Adam couldn't be certain, the man seemed harmless, so he decided to approach him. But it appeared the man already knew he was there.

"I was wondering how long you were planning on hiding," he said, surprising Adam. "They won't bite, you know."

Adam came out from behind the building and walked toward the man who now stood like a scarecrow between the birds. A few pigeons were perched on his outstretched arms picking food from his hands while others patiently waited their turn atop his head. He seemed friendly, so Adam didn't hesitate to approach him.

"Sorry, I didn't mean to intrude," Adam said.

"Oh, it's not every day I get company up here. I assume you're here to fix the vents." He paused, studying Adam's face. "I take it you're not. So? Why are you here?"

Adam didn't quite know how to answer him since he'd never intended his visit to be anything more than fact-finding from a distance.

"I'm interested in your birds."

The man frowned.

"Why?"

Adam's heart skipped a beat. There was something intimidating about this seemingly harmless man that had Adam at a loss for words.

"Who sent you?" the man asked before Adam could answer his previous question.

"No one, I just needed to know if your birds are up for hire."

The man let out a few short whistles and the birds instantly reacted by flying off to a large coop behind him.

"Wow, that's impressive," Adam said in response to their trained obedience.

The man didn't say a word. Instead, he stuck his hands inside his pockets and fixed his gray eyes on Adam's as if he were waiting for Adam to answer an unspoken question. His silent intimidation worked, and Adam found himself suddenly blurting out the truth.

"I found this book that contains pages of pigeon numbers." He pulled the ledger from underneath his shirt and held it up for him to see, then continued. "It's how I tracked you down. I need to know more about it."

Silence followed.

For a moment there, Adam thought of running while he could still get away. There was no telling how this man was involved and what he was capable of. But as before, he couldn't move.

"Are you police?"

"Oh no, no, nothing like that. I'm trying to help a friend. I'm Adam, by the way."

Another deep stare, then the man turned and walked towards the small building and paused just outside the steel door. When he turned and faced Adam, his bushy gray eyebrows were drawn into a frown over his now dark eyes that darted in all directions as if searching for something.

"You can't be here. You need to leave and put that book away."

His words were cloaked in fear, which took Adam by surprise, but he did as he was told.

"I just need a few minutes of your time, to ask you some questions," Adam said as he took a few quick steps towards him.

"No! You need to leave. If they see you here, we're both dead," the bird man barked, his body tense and slightly aggressive as he heaved his chest forward.

"Fine, I'm sorry, I'll go. I didn't mean to upset you," Adam said, holding his hands up in surrender.

The man yanked the steel door to the small building open and stepped inside to shut himself off from Adam, then paused and shouted over his shoulder.

"And don't come back! You don't know what you're getting yourself involved with. Stay away!"

But the warning came too late.

To his right, a single bullet clanked hard against the steel door inches from the man's shoulder.

He flinched.

Adam ducked.

Another bullet whistled through the air and wedged itself between two red bricks to their left.

Then another, just below that.

Now sprawled on the ground, Adam covered his head with his hands. The bird man's frail hand beckoned.

"Get inside!"

Responding to his invitation, Adam crawled toward the building where the man shielded himself behind the steel door moments before another bullet slammed into the steel. The deafening sound sent shock waves through Adam's limbs and he scrambled, desperate to take shelter behind the door.

A quick succession of shots rang through the air. The dull sound of the last bullet clashed with an intense pain that exploded through his entire body and forced Adam face first onto the ground.

CHAPTER EIGHTEEN

On the floor inside the building, locked away behind the steel door, Adam clutched his right shoulder. Blood seeped between his fingers while his mind tried to compute what had just happened. The bird man's arms hooked around his waist and he felt his body being lifted into a chair. As he gazed down at the bleeding wound, he thought he was going to be sick—or pass out. A second later, the man pressed a towel onto the wound and Adam cringed with pain.

"Who else is here?" The bird man asked angrily.

"No one, just me."

"He's not one of them, so either you're lying to me, or someone followed you here."

Adam was certain he'd intentionally pushed down on the towel as he spat the words at him.

"I came alone. No one knows I'm here, I swear."

"You shouldn't have come," the man said and then casually announced, "It's just a graze, you'll be fine."

He turned and kneeled in front of a steel trunk that stood against one of the walls. Adam watched as he flipped the lid, then pulled a gun from between the layers of a black rag. As if he'd done it a million times before he released the magazine into his hands, checked it, and clicked it back in place. With the gun now on the floor next to him, his hands disappeared back inside the chest and Adam watched in stunned silence as he retrieved a box of bullets followed by a black backpack.

Outside their humble fortress, something frightened the pigeons, sending them flapping into flight. It had caught the bird man's attention too, and he was quick to lift a black-and-white picture frame from the wall behind him to reveal a small peephole.

"It's him," he announced in a whisper, dropping the picture frame back in place.

"Who?"

"Whoever you brought here with you."

"Honestly, I didn't bring anyone here with me."

The bird man didn't answer. He had returned to his trunk, from where he retrieved another gun.

Silenced by fear—or perhaps it was curiosity over why this man had a trunk full of guns—Adam hastily studied the room. Much larger than it had appeared from the outside, the red brick structure was quite spacious and surprisingly tidy. In the furthest corner along the back wall was a single bed, its bedding perfectly neat as if it were pressed. A table equipped with a toaster and microwave stood wedged against the wall to his left and opposite that was a black leather recliner with the upholstery foam pushing through in several places.

His eyes moved to the trunk. It was military issue, the white printed number nearly completely rubbed away. Inside the lid, there was a US flag confirming that the bird man must have served at some time.

When the man, whom Adam now noticed was easily in his seventies, shut the trunk and moved to the bed, Adam watched his arthritic hands bury the guns inside his jacket and waistband. He paused, distracted by a noise outside. Adam heard it too, then feet shuffled just on the other side of the wall. He turned around, his index finger across his lips telling Adam not to make a sound. Moments later their shooter was at the steel door. Panic flooded Adam's body, then questions. No one knew he was there. Who'd be shooting at him? Still clasping his bleeding arm, he traced his steps back to the hospital. Stunned at his stupidity, he realized he had left the computer screen open, the building's address exposed. His shooter was in all probability the same man who had tried to kill Patrick and the very man who was now trying to push his way through the bird man's door. He had followed him there.

To his left, the steel door shook in its frame as the shooter attempted to break the bolted door down. There was no other way in, and no way out. As much as the door protected them, it also kept them from escaping.

And as dread gradually increased in Adam's throat, still seated and bleeding from the gunshot wound in his arm, he looked to the old man for answers. But what he got instead was yet another secret that revealed the bird man's mysterious past. Seemingly unperturbed by the vicious banging on the door, Adam stared at the bird man who had pulled away the chocolate brown rug on the floor by his bed to reveal a wooden hatch in the floor.

Armed and now with his backpack on his back, he beckoned to Adam as he opened the hatch.

"Can you move?" he whispered.

Adam nodded.

Below the floor, a shaft just wide enough to hug their shoulders descended into darkness.

"Grab onto the ladder," he mouthed and pointed to the metal ladder that stretched against one side.

Adam didn't hesitate and, with his good arm curled around each rung, his body leaning against the ladder, he lowered himself as quickly as his injury would allow. Above his head the bird man descended, leaving a gap in the hatch just large enough to pull the rug back in place before he lowered and locked the trapdoor back in place.

The escape shaft instantly turned pitch black and Adam felt himself grow wary of continuing into the darkness. But above their heads, the banging continued, soon followed by several gunshots clanging loudly against what he had guessed was the door's lock mechanism.

"Hurry," the bird man pushed, "there's only a few more steps."

He was right, and Adam's feet hit the floor a mere five steps later. With the man now beside him, his flashlight cut through the darkness and Adam watched as the man released the rung locks for the ladder to drop into half its length.

The space was cramped and had them pressed together in the tight underground cavity like sardines in a tin.

"This way." He brushed past Adam, turning his body as if they were dancing until he had shuffled them into position then swiftly, he led them down a narrow underground passage.

"Who are you? What is this place?" Adam said, unable to hold back the million questions that looped in his head.

"I might ask you the same question."

"I told you, I'm Adam. I just needed more information about your birds so I can help a friend."

"Yeah, you said that already. Problem is, I don't believe you."

The tunnel curved to the right.

"It's the truth, though. His name's Patrick and he's

about to be arrested for something I don't believe he did."

"And you're the hero, fighting for justice."

"Yes... no, I just know he didn't do it and it has something to do with the ledger he had on him. I think that's what this guy is after. He tried to kill Patrick earlier this morning."

"So now he's after you, and you're dragging me into your little hero quest."

"I suppose so. Look, I'm sorry, honestly I am. I just need to know why he recorded hundreds of bird numbers in a notebook that's quite evidently important enough to kill for."

The man didn't speak as they turned down another hidden passageway.

"I'll leave you alone if you can just tell me what your birds have to do with everything, please."

The man stopped and turned to face him; the flashlight pinned to Adam's chest.

"It's not just numbers, Adam. It's a manifest of recorded transactions."

He turned and continued down the tunnel.

"A manifest, transactions, are you sure? Of what?"

He stopped again, this time in front of what appeared to be an old elevator.

"If I tell you, will you leave me and my birds alone and not tell anyone how you got this information?"

"Yes, I give you my word."

The man studied his face.

"I hope you mean that, son. These guys aren't the type who play around, they're dangerous. More importantly, they have connections in high places. People like Bill Sutton." He paused, waiting to see Adam's reaction.

"You know about Sutton," Adam said stunned, noting the disdain on the bird man's face.

"I might look like a nobody, Adam, but I'm not an idiot."

He turned and pushed the elevator gate to one side before parting its doors and stepping inside. Adam followed.

"I didn't mean to imply you were an idiot. I'm just surprised that you know about Sutton's death."

The mysterious man closed the gate, then the doors, refraining from pressing the lift's button. He was on his knees, his backpack now on the floor in front of him.

"Take off your jacket."

Adam did as he was told.

The man's aged hands swiftly worked at Adam's wound, disinfecting it, then wrapping it in a bandage.

"It hit the muscle, which is why it's affecting your mobility, but you'll be fine. Graze wounds heal fast. Just keep it clean."

"You seem to know a lot about guns and stuff. Did you serve?" Adam said, hoping the man would answer him.

"Fifteen years in the field and another twenty at base

before they gave me the golden handshake, replaced by 'a younger version', younger and inexperienced alright."

Adam detected the bitterness in his voice.

"You didn't agree with that decision?"

The hurt behind his eyes declared the truth.

"I served this country my entire life, sacrificed my wife, my kids, everything, in exchange for a severance so small I barely have enough to put food on the table. They would've lost many battles had it not been for me and my birds."

"So they are spy birds, actual spy birds."

The man smiled proudly, neither confirming nor denying Adam's speculation.

His fingers yanked at his backpack's zip, closing the bag and with it, Adam's inquiry. Standing with his back towards Adam, he pressed the button and the lift jumped into action.

"The great Dr. Bill Sutton wasn't the upstanding philanthropist the world thinks he was. He was rotten to the core. He might have donated millions to charities and done every good deed known to man, but his soul was as black as the devil himself. Those millions of dollars he so freely gave away, parading it as if he'd earned it through honest hard work were nothing but blood money, literal blood money. He was the prover-bial wolf in sheep's clothing. Whoever that shooter is up there, was in bed with him, and he's closer to home than you might think."

The lift's doors opened and Adam followed him out into an alley that opened up onto the sidewalk behind the building. He reached out as if to shake Adam's hand, but instead deposited something in his palm.

"Watch your six, Adam. You can't trace cryptocurrency, but there is more than one way to skin a cat." He then turned and disappeared around the corner.

CHAPTER NINETEEN

W ith the mysterious bird man's words still ringing in his ears, Adam stared at the object in his hand. Twice folded was a postcard, the corners of which were creased and worn. When he unfolded the postcard, it revealed an image of the Statue of Liberty, standing proudly in the distance. He flipped it over. The back was blank, except for the postage stamp dated three years prior. The date bore no significance to anything Adam could think of, neither did the image. Puzzled by the meaning behind the bird man's clandestine gift that frankly any tourist stand in New York would sell, he stuffed it inside his pocket and headed off in search of food—he had eaten nothing all day and the hunger pangs had already started drowning out the pain in his arm.

As his mind worked ceaselessly to solve the myriad questions that tugged at him, he looked over his shoulder every few strides, just in case the shooter was following him. Near dusk, and conscious of a million invisible eyes on him, he increased his pace, clutching his bad arm firmly against his chest. Two blocks down, he found himself in a slightly better neighborhood and stepped inside the first semi-decent sandwich shop he could find. The tiny shop was crowded, but he managed to find a seat at a table tucked away in the back. The opportunity of a brief respite brought much relief, a chance to drum out the noise and seek a new direction. But all he felt was confusion. He glanced at his watch. He was fast running out of time. For all he knew, they could have already taken Patrick into custody.

With his mind now fully occupied by the day's events, he recalled the bird man's parting words and wondered why he'd warned him about cryptocurrencies and how it all fit with his birds and Patrick.

He'd heard of these digital currencies but had no idea how they worked. Daniel had once mentioned that it was the beginning of the end of the world and it had sparked a three-hour-long dinner conversation about the possibility of it fulfilling biblical prophecy.

Another two bites of his sandwich finished his meal and he washed it down with the last bit of his coffee. He pushed the paper serving basket to one side and signaled for the check. As he waited for it, he took the postcard from his jacket and smoothed it out onto the table. There had to have been a reason the bird man gave it to him—he was far too methodical for it not to mean anything.

His eyes focused on the photo. It wasn't anything different from what he'd seen a million times before. Lady Liberty standing tall in the harbor, surrounded by water against the city backdrop. In the forefront, as if the photographer stood on the banks of the river, a single signpost read Pier 63. Nothing untoward, it seemed.

He turned the postcard over and studied the postage stamp. At first glance, it was nothing different from what he'd seen earlier; a date three years before. But, in the bright glow of the overhead lights, he noticed something he hadn't seen in the dusk light earlier. When angled to one side, the light lit up the pale outlines of an imprint written vertically along the side of the card. Faded and near invisible at a glance, there was no denying it. The writing reminded him of the reddish-brown ink used to decorate the Indian brides during their wedding ceremonies and was so cleverly done it might have been mistaken for a decorative stamp.

His pulse quickened with his discovery, and he turned the card sideways to better read it. Written out alphabetically, joined with no spacing, were the numbers three, eight, five and, two.

With his mind now charged with bolts of enthusiasm, Adam instantly realized the photo on the front of the postcard was directing him to a specific place, and while he didn't quite know what the numbers meant yet, he knew beyond a doubt that the bird man was instructing him to go to Pier 63.

CHAPTER TWENTY

Detective Kane stopped midway through pouring himself another cup of coffee when his boss yelled his name across the office.

"One guess we know what that's about," he said to Jones before he set off to the chief's office.

"Shut the door," the chief barked.

"I know what you're going to say, Chief. I'll have that confession on your desk—" Kane stopped mid-sentence when the chief's eyes warned him he'd assumed incorrectly.

"You wanna know who I just spoke to on the phone, Kane?" It was a rhetorical question Kane knew from experience not to answer.

"That was the mayor, and you wanna know who *he* just got off the phone with?" Another rhetorical question.

"Your old man, that's who, again!"

Kane's shoulders drooped along with his head.

"He stopped being my father a long time ago, Chief."

"Don't give me that attitude, Kane! The man's insane and last time I checked, you guys share the same blood. I can't have him calling up the mayor, planting all sorts of crazy theories in his head. It's enough that I have the mayor all over this Sutton case that you're nowhere near solving. I don't care that you haven't spoken to him in the last five years. Shut him up!"

The chief turned his back on Kane and buried himself in a folder to signal that it wasn't up for further discussion, and Kane promptly returned to his desk.

"That was quick," Detective Jones commented.

"Quick and brutal. My old man's up to his usual conspiracy theory antics. Apparently, he has the mayor up in arms."

He snatched his jacket from the back of his chair.

"You coming?" he invited Jones.

"Do I have a choice? On second thought, perhaps I should, yes, to make sure you and your father don't kill each other this time."

"He's a lunatic, Jonesy. Sometimes I wish he'd died in one of those wars."

"You can't mean that, Kane. Yes, he might have lost a marble or two, but wouldn't you if you had gone through what he did? They don't just hand out purple hearts to every soldier, you know."

"Yeah, well, he had more love for this country than for his own family. America and those stupid birds of his."

WHEN TWENTY MINUTES LATER KANE AND JONES arrived on the rooftop of the building, that had been home to his estranged father for nearly fifteen years, they immediately knew something was wrong. Empty shell casings lay scattered in front of the red brick building along with several bullets that were still lodged in the metal door.

They drew their guns and took shelter behind the building.

As they listened, they heard a metal noise coming from the far end of the roof. They split up. Jones aimed her gun inside the building while Kane set off in the direction of the noise.

"Clear," Jones reported.

When she turned to find her partner, she glimpsed him disappearing over the side of the building. She ran towards him. As she reached the edge of the roof, she found Kane in pursuit of a man fleeing down the external fire escape.

Her hand reached for her radio and she called for reinforcements, charging toward the stairwell.

When Jones finally made it out of the building and around the corner where the fire escape hung down the side of the building, neither Kane nor the intruder were anywhere in sight. Her pulse quickened, her body tense and on full alert, anticipating danger. Then she heard her partner's enraged exclamation from the opposite side of the road. When she met up with him he was furious, his gun holstered and his hands on his hips.

"It's him," he said, gasping for air.

"Who?"

"Our murdering doctor impersonator."

"You mean the guy who tried to kill Phillips."

"Yep, dark eyes, dark hair, six one, muscles to put Popeye to shame."

He paced the curb.

"You think perhaps your father's really involved in something?" Jones asked, but she knew her partner well enough to know he was running the same question through his head.

Kane reached for his cell and allowed his thumb to find his father's number.

It rang. No answer. He rang again but got the same result. His next call was to the office, asking that they put a trace on his father's phone. And as he stood contemplating his next move, his heart was confronted with the reality that his father might actually be in trouble. And although he had a hard time admitting it, he knew his earlier death wish had come from a place of hurt, not hate.

His phone rang, and he promptly answered it. In his ear, the officer's voice pulled his attention back.

"Fine, keep trying and let me know the second you have a location on him," he responded.

"Nothing?" Jones inquired.

"Nope, his phone's off. He must have turned it off after I called."

"Any idea what's going on?"

Kane rubbed his face with both hands and let out a forced laugh.

"No idea, but whatever he's into, has something to do with this case. How Phillips, the hospital killer, and my father are connected beats me, but I'm sure as heck going to push him for answers when I find him."

When their backup arrived, they went up to the roof and set about investigating the scene. Inside his father's humble quarters, Kane allowed his eyes to take it all in. Next to his father's bed, an old photo of the two of them on a fishing trip caught him by surprise. He remembered that trip all too well. His father had just gotten discharged, and he thought it would cheer him up, get his mind off things, ease him into retirement—and restore their broken relationship. Instead, his father had decided he'd rather spend the entire trip drinking and nearly killed himself when he passed out atop the camp-fire. It was the last time they spoke or saw each other.

"You okay?" Jones asked.

"Yeah, fine, see anything?" He turned the conversation back to the case and squatted down next to the army chest on the floor.

"His medals, uniform, and a few empty clips." She lifted the black rag to his face. "Smell this, gunpowder, right?"

Kane nodded.

"Safe to say he had a gun, possibly left in a hurry when this guy came for him. What was this guy looking for? Why come here?"

Kane turned around, still squatted, his eyes searching.

"There's blood." He snapped his fingers, grabbing the attention of a nearby forensic expert. "I need a name, yesterday," he said sternly.

"Think it's his?" Jones said.

"I don't know what to think anymore, Jonesy. It's just like him to get all up in my business."

He swore under his breath and stepped outside. To his right, his father's beloved pigeons sat perched in their coop. Hands on hips, Kane stood staring at them through the fenced wall. As a child, he recalled how jealous he was of them, jealous of the attention they got. So jealous he couldn't stand being near them when they were together. It was stupid; he knew. They were just birds, but his father had chosen them over him anyway, and they chose him. They had been by his side all these years, remained loyal to their keeper. He lived for them, often sat inside the coop with them. It was as if he'd lived in there with them.

A sudden thought snapped into place, and Kane opened the door to step inside.

"What are you doing?" Jones asked, thinking he'd lost his mind.

Kane paused amid the birds.

"I bet you look at these and think they're just ordinary pigeons. They're not. Wanna know what my father did in the military?" He didn't wait for Jones to answer and continued. "He flew these pigeons. They're carrier pigeons, used to send messages between units, even spy behind enemy lines. He was their handler."

"I never knew that." Jones studied her partner's face. "What you thinking, Kane?"

He sat down on the ground between them like he had when he was just a kid.

"I think he's still doing it."

"What, spying? You're saying your father's a spy? That's ridiculous."

Kane didn't answer.

"You said it before, Jonesy. You don't just get purple hearts for doing nothing. He was a war hero back in his day, he nearly died for his country, and that's not something that changes when you retire. From what I heard, he was in deep and if not for his age catching up with him, he'd still be there."

Kane pondered the notion as he soaked up the atmosphere inside the coop. Several pigeons perched on his shoulders and knees as he sat cross-legged. For the most part, they weren't scared of him, as if they sensed he was family. Directly in front of him, one of the larger ones cooed loudly, as if he were desperate for Kane's attention, talking to him.

"Been there, buddy," Kane said, referring to his earlier memories of his own jealousy.

But as Kane's eyes focused on the bird, he spotted the tiny cylinder attached to one leg.

"I knew it!" he said, then instantly calmed himself down so as not to scare the bird away.

"What, what happened?" Jones said from behind the fence, watching as Kane held out his hand to the noisy pigeon in front of him. Almost as soon as he did, the bird walked towards him, then jumped onto his hand. Ten seconds later Kane had the cylinder off the pigeon's leg and in his hand. He found himself thanking the pigeon just like his father would do and watched it hop off and walk away. Kane thought it odd that he didn't fly off as was the norm, and he summoned the bird with a rhythmic whistle that caught Jones by surprise.

"I've learned more about you in the past two days than I have in the five years we've been together, Kane."

"Interesting," he mumbled under his breath as he spread the bird's wings out.

"What is?"

"His wings have been clipped."

"Okay?"

"He can't fly, Jonesy, so why would he be carrying a message if he can't deliver it?"

"Maybe your father forgot to take it off?"

"Not a chance. My father neglected a lot of things in his life, but neglecting one of his birds was never one of them."

Kane put the bird down and turned his attention back to the small metal cylinder. The size and shape of a large medicine capsule, he lifted the top off and pulled the scrolled paper from the cavity.

CHAPTER TWENTY-ONE

S till seated in the center of the pigeon coop, Kane hovered over the tiny paper scroll he had just uncovered.

"What's it saying?" Jones prompted.

"Everything and nothing."

Jones clicked her tongue in annoyance.

"That makes no sense, Kane, spit it out."

Kane got to his feet and joined his partner outside the pigeon loft. Handing her the scrolled piece of paper, he turned away to hide the emotion that suddenly lay bare in his face.

Surprised by her partner's uncharacteristic display of emotions, Jones unrolled the piece of paper.

"It just says Pier 63. I don't understand. As far as I know, that place has been deserted for years. What's gotten you so emotional about it?"

Kane turned to face his partner.

"I haven't seen my father in years, yet he knew that one day, somehow, I'd be up here to find that cylinder. This bird's wings have been clipped for one reason only, so he can't fly off. I used to sit in the coop like this when I was a kid. I used to love hanging out with them while he was away. My father knew that, remembered that. He had every intention of me finding this message."

"I think that's pretty cool. Any reason why he wanted you to find it?"

He shook his head as one of the forensic investigators came towards him.

"We got a match on the blood sample, Detective," she said and handed him a printout.

He scanned the page, then smirked.

"Now isn't that interesting? It seems the pastor is more involved in this than we thought."

"The pastor? You mean the guy who found Phillips?"

"One and only, and if I recall, also the one who claimed he saw our hospital killer moments after he tried to murder our primary suspect."

"This case keeps getting more complicated by the minute. Who would've thought a pastor was tangled up in all of this?"

"Not to mention why he'd be bleeding all over my father's floor."

A moment later Kane's phone rang.

"Kane," he answered, then instantly reacted to the caller.

"You can't be serious, Chief! The man's guilty as sin. I understand, but there has to be something we can do, at least have a chance to interview the man properly."

He went quiet, then ended the call.

"Tell me the Feds didn't get their way," Jones guessed.

"Worse, they let Phillips go. Our dear friend William Sutton lawyered up. We've got nothing to hold him on. You were right, all circumstantial. The chief wants us back to complete the paperwork."

He tucked the piece of paper inside his jacket pocket and turned to leave.

"I'll go, you go meet your father at the pier," Jones offered. "And call for backup if you see anything suspicious. Don't be a hero," she added over her shoulder as she flagged down one of the other officers for a lift back to the office.

It wasn't the smack across his face that agitated Patrick, neither was it the pain caused by the chafing of the tight cord around his hands. Nothing could have hurt more than the sting of betrayal.

Seated in a corner on William's apartment floor, he lifted his throbbing head and stared his long-time friend full in the face.

"I'm waiting, Patrick, where is the ledger?"

"I already told you, I don't have it anymore. It must have washed away when I almost drowned in the middle of a hurricane." Patrick couldn't hide the contempt he felt.

"Not likely, buddy. Why did you take it anyway, huh? How much more are they paying you? I mean, one would've thought, after everything we did for you and your family, I'd at least have some loyalty in return. But no, your greed got the better of you. You just couldn't help yourself. You know, my father was going to get rid of you. But then I bet you already knew that, didn't you? That's why you stole that ledger, to blackmail my father."

Patrick's insides shrank into a tight ball.

"It wasn't anything like that, William. I wouldn't do that, I didn't do that."

William paced the floor in front of him, his hands on his hips, his body slumped forward.

"You've always thought you're smarter than me. Everything was so easy for you. School, the girls, heck even your career. I stood by you, Patrick! When you lost your parents, I made sure you were okay, handed

Gencorp to you on a silver platter. How could you steal from us, huh? How was it that all we did wasn't enough for you?" He went down on his haunches and pinned his freckled face directly in front of Patrick's. "Well, I don't believe a word you're saying. I think you know exactly where that ledger is. I might have not liked my father much, but I will not let that ledger drag my family's name through the mud. My father might be dead, but I have a chance to turn this around and protect my mother's name. That ledger will destroy her and bring shame upon this family. I won't let it. I won't let you ruin our name by exposing my father's mistakes for the entire world to blow out of proportion. I have my legacy to protect, and it will be a sad day on earth if I let you take that away from me."

He rose without giving Patrick a chance to speak and walked across the room to where his cellphone lay on the kitchen counter. He seemed anxious, almost as if he didn't quite know what to do. William's fingers glided over his phone before he pressed it against his ear, his back towards Patrick.

"It's me. He says he lost it at sea. I don't know, but he can't stay here. Yes, I know where that is."

William popped the phone in his pocket and turned to face Patrick.

"Get up, we're taking a little trip to the pier. Let's see how quickly you remember where the journal is when we throw you overboard again."

CHAPTER TWENTY-TWO

Cloaked in a blanket of darkness, Pier 63 was deserted and eerily quiet. The view from the pillared structure that stretched out into the bay made for the perfect vantage point of the iconic statue that stood watch over the city. Adam ignored the sign that told trespassers to keep out and climbed over the low-hanging chain. At the end of the pier, the small, rusted carcass of a once used passenger ferry bobbed in the water. A sudden chill came upon him as he neared it— there wasn't a soul in sight. He stood watching the boat, cringing at the screeching sounds emitted from the hull scraping against exposed metal. Higher up a door banged rhythmically along with the gentle swaying of the boat.

He turned his body in a circle, surveying the dark, empty space around him, and questioned whether to step on board, whether it was safe. In the distance behind him, drifting on the gentle breeze, he heard the no entry chain rattle, its rusty bolts screeching as it swung back and forth. Apart from the ferry, there was nowhere to hide. Alert, with his heart thumping against his chest, he crouched down, thinking it might be security doing a quick check from a distance.

He was wrong.

From the shadows, he saw a man's figure walk towards him, the boardwalk planks creaking with each step. Slight panic set in as the man came closer.

Adam's eyes scanned the side of the boat. Attached to its hull was a rusty ladder, illuminated under the only light—the moon's reflection on the water. He was still contemplating it when the man's voice told him to identify himself. Stunned, Adam remained quiet. Again the voice hollered at him, then announced he was NYPD.

Adam relaxed, knowing his only crime was trespassing—easily explainable as a touristy error in judgment.

Adam raised his hands above his head in surrender.

"Sorry, officer, I'm not looking for any trouble."

The man was upon him.

Kane's eyes narrowed as the trespasser's face came into view. Unclipping his holster, his hand settled in position on his firearm. Then he recognized him.

"You! What the… actually, I shouldn't be surprised.

Keep your hands where I can see them," Kane instructed Adam.

Adam complied.

"What are you doing here, Pastor? Where's my father?"

The frown on Adam's face told Kane there was more than one question running through his mind too.

"I don't understand, your father?" Adam said, puzzled.

"Quit playing games. I know you were with him." Kane scanned Adam's body for the wound that had left the blood evidence.

"I'll ask you again, where's my father?"

"Look, officer, I don't know who you're referring to. I think you might have me mistaken—"

"Save it, there's no mistake! Your blood is all over his floor. And it's Detective Kane, by the way."

Adam's mind slowly pieced it together.

"The bird man's your father? I can explain, actually, we're on the same side, Detective. My name's Adam. I'm the one who found Patrick on our beach. He's not your man."

Kane didn't react and kept his vigilant stance. He knew who he was. He recalled seeing Adam in Patrick's room after the attempt on his life and had been told he was the pastor who'd found him and brought him in.

Adam continued.

"Yes, I was with your father, I was led to him, actually. He saved me from getting my head blown off, but he left the second we got out of the building. He gave me this, that's how I found my way here." Adam held out the postcard.

When Kane inspected the image under his flashlight and saw it carried the same instruction his father had given him, he allowed his body to relax.

"Why would he send us both here?" Kane mused.

"He sent you here too?"

Kane showed him the paper.

"It was concealed on one of his pigeons."

There was a noise coming from inside the boat and Kane looked up to inspect the ferry. "Who else is here?"

"I don't know, I just got here."

Something in the way Kane looked out across the water told Adam that Detective Kane was as confused as he was. Deciding to trust him, he told him all that had happened and had led to that moment, how he knew God wanted him to help Patrick, and that he believed with all his heart that he was innocent. And while Kane didn't share in the same conviction—or faith—he didn't argue. Every part of him so desperately needed to find the truth, to protect his father.

BROUGHT TOGETHER BY TWO FORCES NEITHER OF THEM had control over, Adam and Kane resolved to seek the truth together, each one propelled by their own inner calling, each one not wanting to disappoint their father. And although their worlds were realms apart, they were required to equally trust all the same.

It was Kane who climbed the ladder that stretched out against the ferry's hull first. When he was sure there was no one else around, he motioned for Adam to join him. They followed the sound of the rhythmic slamming of the steel door as it led them around the deck to the front of the boat. With Kane's hand firmly on his holster, ready to draw, they quietly moved in on the door and paused just outside it.

"You ready?" Kane whispered.

Adam nodded, unsure if he truly was.

Beyond the steel door, the narrow passageway was consumed in the near pitch-black darkness. Only slightly muffled by the screeching noises of the boat, their hearts beat loudly in their chests. At the end of the short passageway, they came to another door, equal in size and fabric. But unlike the previous one, this one was shut, locked in place by an electronic pin pad. A few tugs left Kane perplexed and unsuccessful, so he aimed his gun at the lock.

"No, wait!" Adam said, "I think I have the code."

Kane's expression queried how.

"I need your flashlight," Adam whispered, ready with the postcard in hand.

He entered the henna numbers into the digital lock. The lock released, and the door sprang open.

Now on full alert, gun drawn and firmly braced against his chest, Kane proceeded, Adam close behind him. Senses fully alert, eyes peeled into the darkness, the pair found themselves at the top of a steel staircase that led them down into the belly of the beast. Hearing no sound to show they weren't alone, Kane shone his flashlight across the floor, his gun aimed ahead and resting atop it. Their feet echoed in the hollow space while their eyes took in the horror that unfolded with each step they took. Cubicles made from large sheets of frosted plastic hung from the roof. The smell of rotten flesh hung thick in the air, forcing them both to cover their noses.

"What is this place?" Adam said from behind the crook of his elbow. "Smells like a morgue."

"That's because it is, in a matter of speaking."

And while Adam didn't quite yet comprehend, Kane knew precisely what they had found. As he pulled one of the sheets away, his suspicions were confirmed when, in the center of the cubicle, a mutilated body greeted them. Disgust overwhelmed Adam's senses and he almost turned and ran off the boat. On the floor beneath the body, there were pools of dried blood, no more than a few days old if Kane had to guess. To one side a blue and white cooler similar in size to a six-pack of beer stood on a steel table. The sticker on it warned it contained biohazard material. He reached for the lid and opened it. It was empty but ready to receive new contents.

"Please tell me this isn't what I think it is," Adam pleaded.

"I'm afraid it is. It seems we find ourselves smack bang in the middle of an organ trafficking facility."

He moved across to the next partition; it was empty, clean and sterile. So were the three others next to that. But in the sixth and final one, the same gruesome scene greeted them.

"This is disgusting," Adam declared, his heart heavy with hurt and appalled by the sinful nature of humankind. "I've read about these things, but I guess a part of me was in denial. I never thought I'd ever experience the truth first-hand."

Kane walked to face him.

"You okay?"

Adam nodded. He needed to be. In his head, he begged God to numb his heart, to help him not to judge, to pray against this evil, to pray for their souls.

And as he followed Kane back inside the first cubicle, watched him reach for his phone to call it in, the hollow crime scene suddenly echoed with male voices coming down the stairs in the distance behind them.

Quick to react, Kane killed his flashlight, pointed his firearm towards the voices. Adam froze in place, listened, was thankful for the darkness that concealed them. But no sooner had the thought filled his mind than the entire chamber lit up like a Christmas tree. With their shadows now putting them at risk of being discovered, Adam and Kane crouched down underneath the steel table, concealed only by a bloodstained green surgical sheet that hung halfway down the side of the table. Kane's gun was ready to shoot, his mind sharp, his senses alert. At first, all he heard were footsteps accompanied by subdued male voices, but as the men drew closer, and the voices became clearer, there was no mistaking it.

One voice, in particular, gripped at Kane's heart and tore it into a thousand pieces. And almost simultaneously, it had done the same with Adam. When their eyes met and exchanged a silent conversation, Adam and Kane agreed that the voice belonged to Kane's father.

CHAPTER TWENTY-THREE

Feeling as if someone had just punched him in the gut, Kane couldn't function. In the deepest corners of his fenced-in heart, he had secretly hoped his father wouldn't be involved in anything as evil as this. But there had been many years of strain between them and the sudden realization that he'd never really known his father hit home. With his exposed heart now bruised and renewed with a lifetime of pain and disappointment, all hope of reconciling with his father was lost in that very instant.

One of the men with a thick Asian accent spoke.

"You sure this bird of yours will find its way back? We only have one shot at this and you better not blow it. This one's got a big ticket attached to it."

"I'm sure," the bird man replied. "This isn't my first rodeo, Sushruta."

"But it is the first time using this bird, and I'm very certain you said the last one knew its way too. That one nearly cost me millions."

"This one won't get lost."

"Let's hope you're right, I'd hate to take matters into my own hands."

The man of Asian descent barked something in his native language, evidently to someone else. Adam recognized it to be Bangla, the language spoken in Bangladesh. He knew because they'd recently had a Bengali missionary pass through town and stay over at The Lighthouse. The thought suddenly had him curious, wondering if perhaps God had lined it up for this very reason.

Adam and Kane heard someone pass nearby, just outside their cubicle. They froze, their bodies tense, their hearts racing. Almost directly behind them, from within the adjacent cubicle, they felt a man's presence, separated only by the thin layer of frosted plastic sheeting. They heard the rustling noise of one of the plastic curtains being pulled away, then promptly slide back into place. The man reported something in their shared language to the man called Sushruta.

Then suddenly the boat started moving, nearly knocking Adam against the steel table.

"You know the drill, Walter. Get the cage."

Again footsteps came toward them. This time Kane

knew they were his father's; distinct because of the slight dragging in his left leg where he had once sustained a shrapnel injury to his knee. To his left, Kane spotted the empty wicker bird carrier on the floor next to him. His heart stopped. Reality struck. He wanted to run, wasn't ready to face his father, wanted the floor to make him disappear.

But it was too late. The sheeting parted and, from behind the partially opened curtain, his father's once robust frame that now seemed fragile and tired appeared. Three paces toward him, Walter bent down to get the bird carrier from the floor next to him. Their eyes met. Neither said a word. Instead, Kane realized that their presence came as no surprise to his father as if he'd expected them to be there. Walter's eyes appeared warm, gentle, grateful.

Ignoring them, Walter pulled the cloth sheet down lower to better conceal their presence.

"I want a quick exchange, got it?" Sushruta said when Walter returned with the basket.

Walter didn't answer. Moments later the three men's feet were heard shuffling back towards the exit. The lights shut off; the door slammed shut behind them.

When Kane was certain they'd left, he climbed out from underneath the steel table. Adam followed.

This time it was Adam who asked if Kane was okay. Kane nodded and said,

"I wasn't prepared for that, that's all."

Adam surveyed his face under the dim light of Kane's flashlight that now beamed across the partitioned room.

"Your father isn't one of them, Detective. Don't assume the worst."

"You seem very sure of that, Adam. Why is that?"

"I know people, and his heart isn't evil enough to do this. There has to be another reason why he's involved in smuggling human cargo."

Kane studied Adam's face. He was right. His father must have planned it all, set him up to be there. Every last little detail. From the call to the mayor which he knew full well would result in him being sent to shut his father up, to the bird's freshly clipped wings and the address of the pier. It was all intentional, methodically planned out. He knew that now.

"What should we do now?" Adam asked, still aware of the boat moving further away from the dock.

"We go along for the ride and get a closer look at what they're up to. Stay here."

"Where are you going?" Adam whispered.

Kane ignored him.

"I'm not staying behind with all these dead bodies. I don't have the stomach for it," Adam said as he followed Kane, who didn't look too eager to drag him along.

"Fine, but you stay close, got it?"

Adam wasn't going to argue. He'd take his chances following the evildoers over hiding amongst butchered corpses any day.

THE TWO MEN MADE THEIR WAY BACK UP THE LADDER and through the previously locked door. Up ahead they heard the men's voices echo between the steel walls, then a door slammed shut and the space around them went quiet. Adam could no longer control his rapid heartbeat, but he stuck close on Kane's heels as agreed. Kane's gun was back in his hand, his arm extended in line with his shoulder, his movements quick and stealthy. On either side of them, several rusted steel doors lined the narrow corridor, a few squeaking at the hinges as they passed by. Kane held his ear against the first one, listening for voices, movement.

Nothing.

With caution, his hand turned the steel handle, and he peered inside. It was a small utility room. He moved on to the next one. Again he listened, thought he heard movement inside. His back straightened against the wall just outside the door. He readied his body. Adam followed suit. With one quick movement, Kane had the door open and his gun stretched out in front of him, aimed into the darkness. He heard a shuffle, perhaps a groan. His thumb hit the 'on' switch on his flashlight and it lit up the small space inside. Easily identifiable by the two cots on top of each other as being a berth, he saw the curled-up body of a man on the lower bunk. Closer inspection yielded they had tied his hands behind his back, his feet by the ankles. It was Adam who thought he recognized him first.

"Patrick?"

He rushed towards him, and turning his face to the light, confirmed it. Across his mouth was a thick strip of duct tape. He yanked it off.

"It's okay, buddy, we got you," Adam said as he started at the knots around his wrists.

When Kane was certain they weren't in danger, he shut the door behind them and worked the knots around Patrick's ankles.

"You okay?" he whispered.

"I think so."

As they helped him up, his eyes met Adam's.

"You seem to be saving me from these situations a lot lately."

Adam smiled.

"Only doing what I'm supposed to."

Kane interrupted. "Sorry to intrude on your little reunion, but we're somewhat at risk of being caught here, so care to tell me how you ended up here instead of behind bars?"

"William's lawyer. I thought he was on my side,

believed in my innocence. You have to believe me, I didn't steal from Bill or Gencorp, not a dime, and I certainly didn't kill him. I did nothing wrong, Detective."

Kane moved away from the door where he'd been keeping watch.

"What does he think you stole?"

"I found Bill, in his study. He was already dead. The killer came back, so I hid and found a notebook on the floor. It was just lying there, so I took it. Turns out it's why the killer came back. So I ran, fled on the boat, capsized in the storm. I guess that's when I lost it. For some reason, William wants the book, and he thinks I've hidden it somewhere." He dropped his head. "I can't believe he killed his own father."

Kane was back at the door, listening for anyone coming. Satisfied they were still safe, he looked back at Patrick.

"What makes you think William killed his father?"

Patrick looked confused.

"He must have if he's come after me to get the notebook back. How else did he know I had it?"

"So you saw his face, when he came back for it?" Kane pushed.

"No, the man wore a mask. In fact, he seemed much shorter than William now that I think of it."

"What was in the notebook?" Kane asked.

"Just a bunch of random numbers."

"Actually, I can help with that," Adam interrupted, then looked at Patrick. "I'm sorry, Patrick, I took it off you, after we got you off the boat. It was attached to your coat. I shouldn't have, I'm sorry. We were just trying to find out who you were so we could let your family know."

"So you have the notebook?" Kane enquired.

"I do, and it's not just a bunch of numbers. It's a manifest of transactions. That's how I found your father."

At first, Adam thought of telling him where he had hidden it, but a silent whisper told him not to.

"What do you mean it's a manifest?" Kane asked.

"Just that, it's not a random sequence of meaningless numbers. It's pigeon identity codes, a manifest of trans-actions between the US and several other countries."

Kane frowned as he took it all in. After years on the force and a string of successful cases behind him, his bright mind started to piece it together. And suddenly he knew that all the phone calls his father had made to the chief, claiming he had proof of a syndicate smuggling human body parts into the country, were true. Walter knew. He knew because they were using his pigeons to carry messages between the transacting parties.

"So William's on the boat too," Kane said, again nervously listening at the door.

"Not sure. He brought me onto the boat, tied me up,

and left me in here. I didn't see or hear anyone else either while in here."

"Any idea where we're going?" Adam asked.

"Afraid not, but having had my fair share of the ocean's wrath, I'd really like to get off."

"No chance of that happening just yet. Someone's coming," Kane warned.

CHAPTER TWENTY-FOUR

The berth was tiny, with few ways to hide three grown men. They had stuck the duct tape back on Patrick's mouth, loosely wrapped the ropes around his hands and feet, and laid him back on the bed. Kane got into the top bunk, his body pinned against the wall, while Adam hid underneath the bottom bunk. The footsteps grew closer. They barely breathed. When the handle turned and the door opened, Adam's eyes were pinched closed, his soul in prayer. In contrast, Kane lay waiting, his gun ready to fire. Just about noticeable from the view of his top bunk, a man walked in and bent down to check on Patrick. Even with just the dim light from the passage streaming into the cabin, Kane recognized him immediately; it was the same man he had chased after at his father's rooftop abode.

The man spoke perfect American English and instructed Patrick to swing his feet down over the side of the bed. Adam watched from under the bed as the man's knife sliced through the ropes around Patrick's feet. Relieved that he didn't notice it had already been loosened, he thanked his protector for helping them. They watched in horror as the man pulled Patrick to his feet and shoved him toward the door. Seconds later they disappeared into the dimly lit corridor and the door slammed shut behind them.

It took Kane hardly any time to jump off the cot and rush to the door, Adam almost equally fast. Neither spoke when Kane quietly opened the door and peered outside. Patrick's captor led them down another corridor, and they disappeared around the corner. Kane beckoned for Adam to follow.

With the stealth of two lions gaining on their prey, they wasted no time in following them, thankful when they easily stuck to their trail.

The man had a gun shoved between Patrick's shoulder blades, pushing him to walk faster, barking at the back of his head. Another few steps and they ascended a small set of steel steps to the deck. Close on their heels, Kane and Adam followed, pausing on the steps just below the exit. They heard voices. Kane recognized William's. It made his skin crawl. He'd known he was up to something the moment he'd interviewed him. It made him angry, brought to the surface how he felt about entitled rich kids. But he pushed it aside, focused on the job he had to do.

From beneath the short staircase cavity, he popped his head above the deck. Even with several lights fully illuminating the entire deck, he couldn't see them. The voices continued.

On the deck and to his right was a large stack of crates under a brown tarp. He told Adam to wait on the stairs, then shot across the deck and hid between the crates under the tarp. His heart pumped a fresh dose of adrenaline through his body and he paused to contain himself. From his position, the tarp's silver eyelets allowed him to gain sight of the men. There were three that he could see. Sushruta, well-dressed in a black business suit, the hospital killer with his thick tattooed neck looking like he was keeping watch, and William. His father was nowhere to be seen or heard. Annoyed with his limited visibility, he carefully shuffled his body in line with one of the other eyelets. This time he could see his father, standing to one side with his bird carrier held up against his chest. Suddenly there was another male voice. One he hadn't heard before. Again Kane stretched his body over a crate, moving the tarp ever so slightly to try and see his face.

Come on, move to the left, he kept repeating in his mind, willing it telepathically. But the man didn't move. So he tuned his hearing to capture his words.

At first, the voice was gentle, but in a condescending

way. He asked Patrick for the ledger. Kane heard Patrick telling them he'd lost it at sea. The man's voice grew louder, more impatient. But Patrick stuck to his story. After his last denial, the guy with the tattoos drove his fist into Patrick's stomach. Again the man asked for the ledger, then William repeated it as if to emphasize he was in charge too. It reminded Kane of a chihuahua, quick to bark but slow to bite. It must have evoked a reaction from the man as William suddenly raised his hands in surrender and backed away. With a pecking order in place, the man asked Patrick again. His answer remained the same. Once more the tattooed killer stepped forward, preparing to inflict another beating. Walter's voice cut through the air and stopped him before he could deliver the punch, surprising Kane with his father's bravery.

"You might want to pause for now, it's time," Walter said firmly.

Time for what? Kane thought.

From beneath the tarp, Kane watched them yank Patrick aside and make him sit against one of the metal posts, the tattooed man's dark eyes upon him. At that moment, Adam darted across the deck and joined Kane under the tarp.

"I thought I told you to wait there," Kane whispered, annoyed.

"Sorry, I thought they were heading back downstairs. What's happening?"

Adam squeezed his face against one of the eyelets.

"We're about to find out."

Sushruta had a pair of night vision binoculars to his eyes and was scanning the sea. Walter's hand moved inside the bird carrier, which was perched atop a table, released a fistful of birdseed, then flashed a small torch-light as if sending a message via Morse code. He repeated the action a few times: feeding, then flashing. Next, he cupped his hands together over his mouth, curled his fingers to form a chamber, aligned his thumbs and blew into his hands. A loud whistling sound left his hands and echoed out across the ocean.

"What's he doing?" Adam whispered.

"He's calling his bird, directing him to the cage."

A familiar warmth flooded Kane's body as it reminded him of when his father had taught him how to do it when he was a child. He longed to have those moments back.

Less than a minute later the homing pigeon's flapping wings sounded through the air and they watched in awe as he came in to land on top of the cage. Walter removed something from around the bird's neck and handed it to Sushruta. It was a small piece of paper similar to the one Kane had found in the capsule earlier.

"I told you he'd find his way back," Walter boasted, his heart filled with pride over his bird's achievement— and somewhat relieved.

Sushruta ignored his comment. Not that he seemed

like the type of person who'd hand out praise in any event. After he read the note, he made a call from his cellphone.

"We're ready, three hundred and fifty thousand dollars US. Bitcoin."

When he ended the call, he moved to retrieve a laptop from a bag nearby and opened it up on the table. His fingers hit the keys, then inserted what appeared to be a flash drive. Moments later, he removed it and handed it back to Walter.

"Send the payment, and Walter, let's hope this bird is as good as his little friend here."

Walter didn't react. From a second carrier that stood nearby, he attached the computer accessory to another pigeon who had patiently been waiting his turn.

"What's he doing?" Adam asked Kane.

"My guess is he's sending the payment via a cryptocurrency hardware wallet, completely untraceable to its owner and only accessible with a unique password. It's genius," Kane explained.

"So, Sushruta's the middleman, and your father's a pawn."

Kane nodded.

They continued observing the transaction from behind the tarp. So engrossed were they in watching the bird fly off with the payment that they didn't hear the footsteps approach behind them.

Caught off guard with no time for Kane to draw his weapon, they were suddenly staring down the barrel of the tattooed killer's gun.

"Don't even think about it," he said to Kane when he went for his gun. "Slide it over, slowly," he commanded.

Kane did as instructed.

"Now put your hands on top of your heads."

Adam and Kane obeyed.

When the tattooed man was satisfied he had the situation under control, he yelled out across the boat.

"Hey, boss, we've got ourselves some nosy parkers."

The man whose face they couldn't see came toward them and under the dim deck lighting above their heads, he came into full view. Dressed in a gray suit and wearing no tie, his hair was short and bleached, his roots revealing his natural color as brown. His eyes were piercing blue, almost like glass, his nose aristocratic. Neither Kane nor Adam recognized him. Close on his heels was William, who rushed past him.

"Well, isn't this an unexpected surprise," William said when he saw who they had caught.

"Wish I could say the same, Sutton. I knew you were a despicable human being when I first saw you. I'm sure you made your father very proud," Kane said, his words dripping with sarcasm.

"My father... " He gave a cynical laugh. "You know nothing, Kane," William spat back, already battling to control his short temper, his freckled face flushed with anger, his lips pulled into a thin white line.

"Wills, shut your mouth, say nothing else," the white-haired man cautioned, but William continued, his temper now running wild with his emotions.

"You and the rest of the world think you all knew my father. The great Dr. Bill Sutton who went around saving sick people, donating millions, a real saint, like he was Mother Teresa or someone. Well, guess what? He wasn't. Behind his seemingly spotless image, hiding behind all the good work he did for society, he was a miserable excuse for a father, and an even worse human being who abused everything medicine stands for. Do you think I'm here doing this for myself?"

"That's enough, Wills, let it go," the man with the bleached hair said again, his arm stretched out across William's chest.

But all the caution did was fuel William's temper even more.

"No, Mikey, I will not let this go. All my life I've had to carry this pretentious burden around with me. I'm tired of everyone thinking my father was a good Samaritan, and that he was so innocent. It's time the world knew who my father really was, even if these guys aren't going to live to tell the truth."

"You've said too much. I'll handle them," Mikey

said again, his face stern as his muscular hand gripped William's arm.

"What, like you handled getting the ledger? If you'd done your job properly, none of this would have happened. And while I'm at it, let's not forget, you work for me now, not the other way around."

CHAPTER TWENTY-FIVE

When William turned back around to face Adam and Kane, it was the sound Mikey's gun made when he cocked it and aimed it at William's back that caught them all by surprise. Most of all, William.

He turned to face Mikey.

"What do you think you're doing?"

Mikey didn't answer. The sadistic smirk that came over his face declared it all.

"Well, what do you know? Just when I thought I had it all figured out," Kane said.

William's eyes were pinned on the snub-nosed revolver pointed at his face. He instantly recognized it. It was the one he had bought off the bouncer at the club. The very one that went missing when he got mugged.

Mikey's eyes revealed William had caught on.

"Yes, you're right. This is your gun. So now what,

huh? Isn't this just turning out to be the perfect plan? Better than I could've dreamed up, really."

When William spoke, his temper had left him. Instead, his voice portrayed the dumbfounded lack of emotion that came when one tries to piece a situation together.

"Put the gun down, Mikey," he tried.

Mikey laughed.

"Let me think about that for a second." He cocked his head to one side, mocking him, then said, "Yeah, not going to. I think I'm done taking orders from you or anyone else in your family. I've been waiting for this day for a very long time. All these years I was your father's minion, risking life and limb so he could make millions and look good to anyone who cared. And now you swoop in wanting to end it all? Not going to happen, dear Wills. Sit down!"

He waved the tip of the gun toward Adam and Kane, instructing William to sit down next to them.

"So you're going to kill the whole lot of us?" William said, refusing to sit down.

Mikey scoffed.

"Not me, you."

"I'm not killing anyone!" William said, his temper threatening to erupt again.

"Oh, but you see, Wills, you are. This is your gun, remember? An illegally obtained one but, nonetheless, forensics will find your fingerprints all over it. The bouncer, who's on my payroll, by the way, will testify that you bought it from him. And of course, I made sure there's irrefutable surveillance footage to back it up. It will seem as if you killed them in a transaction gone wrong, you and your precious family name will take the fall, and when they find your body with a bullet from the same gun buried in your brain, they'll assume you turned the gun on yourself, guilt-ridden over what you've done, and not able to live with the shame it's caused your family. And I disappear into the sunset with all the blood money your father made. Like I said, it's the perfect plan."

"Except you'd still need to get rid of us," Kane said. "Dead bodies have a way of coming up to the surface after you dump them in the ocean," he added. "Bet you didn't think of that, did you?"

Mikey's smirk turned to a frown. The detective was right. His plan hadn't included a cop and his cronies. The bodies would float. He paused for a moment, contemplating the situation.

"Not if there's none of it left, you idiot."

He looked back over his shoulder where his middleman stood quietly a few steps in front of Walter.

"I reckon we can fetch a fair price for their kidneys, not to mention Patrick's piercing blue eyes. What do you think, Sushruta?"

Sushruta didn't answer.

Mikey repeated his question.

"Hey, you deaf? I'm telling you to pick up the phone and call our clients. The quicker we get rid of this bunch, the sooner we can get on with business."

Still Sushruta didn't answer.

When his body suddenly thrust forward and his hands rose in surrender above his head, Mikey knew there was one person he hadn't considered would foil his perfect plan.

"Put the gun down, Mikey, and tell your minion there to do the same."

Walter shoved his gun deeper into Sushruta's back. He flinched.

"Don't be stupid, Walter. You can retire a rich man," Mikey said.

"I don't want to be rich, Mikey. Money means nothing to me. You've already robbed me of everything that was once precious to me. Put the gun down and let them go."

"You made the choice, old man, not me. You knew what you were getting yourself into, and you profited greatly from it."

Walter's eyes narrowed where he stood shielding behind Sushruta.

"That's where you're wrong, Mikey. I didn't have a choice. None of this was what I wanted. I didn't choose for my wife to get sick. I gave my life to this country and when I needed them to come through for my wife, they refused her treatment. What was I supposed to do, huh? Turn down Bill's offer of a free kidney transplant? So I did what any husband would do to save his wife. I didn't think he'd kill her. You knew the kidney wasn't a match before the transplant. She was your guinea pig, your experiment to see if your scheme would work. But even that wasn't good enough for you. You knew I would rather die than give up my only son, so you bargained with his life too. But, no more. This ends here. I still have a chance to make things right with him, start over."

He paused, the tone of his voice turning cold. "Put down the guns and let them go, or I'll kill Sushruta. Without him, this entire syndicate of yours will come tumbling down like a house of cards."

Walter's gun was now on Sushruta's temple. his eyes stern and locked with Mikey's.

"You think you have it all figured out, don't you, Walter? Do you think I care about *him*? Sushruta was nothing when I found him on the streets of Bangladesh. I built him, created him, heck even gave him a name. He's nothing but a pawn in my masterful game of chess. Just like you. I don't need him any more than I need any of you. Now drop your gun and give it up."

With the gun now pointed at Walter and the tension building to an outcome that would only result in death, Adam could no longer be silent. He had kept one piece of information to himself. Information that he knew would change everything.

"There's only one thing you're forgetting in this evil plan of yours, Mikey," he said, instantly succeeding in breaking the tense standoff.

"Save it, holy man. I don't care about the mumbo jumbo you guys believe in."

"You will. That privilege is reserved for God to show you the truth when he sees fit, Mikey," Adam fearlessly continued. "But I bet you care about the ledger." He paused, waiting for Mikey to react.

"You have the ledger?" William said in disbelief, struggling to keep up with what was slowly unfolding before him.

"I do, and now I know why the two of you are so desperate to get your hands on it. Albeit not for the same reasons."

"What are you doing, Adam?" Kane whispered beside him. Years of police training had taught him not to divulge all his cards, especially not the only evidence they had to build a solid case.

Adam ignored him and continued.

"William's reason I can understand. You knew of your father's evil scheme, and destroying the ledger will destroy all evidence of your father's involvement, protect his legacy, your family name. Your father was clearly a very smart man, William. So smart that he made sure no one could point a finger at him, even with the ledger. To the untrained eye, it's nothing but a book full of digits, ring numbers of the birds. That's what I initially thought too. I even figured out the routes these birds fly. But there was something else I figured out, and I only just realized it a few minutes ago. It's been niggling at the back of my mind. There was an extra digit included in each of those ring numbers. Put them all together and it's the password to Bill's Bitcoin wallet. I bet it's worth a pretty fortune, isn't it, Mikey? That's why you killed him."

The information stunned everyone into silence.

Mikey's eyes narrowed, his face angry.

"*You* killed my father?" William said when the full extent of Mikey's betrayal became clear.

"Your father was an idiot, Wills. He suddenly had an attack of morality and wanted to clear his conscience, donate everything in the hope it would save his soul. All because someone had told him his good work wouldn't secure his entry to heaven. What a bunch of hogwash! But no matter what I said, I couldn't change his mind. There was no way I was going to let him walk out on this operation and take all the money with him."

William struggled to contain his emotions that now ran wild with anger as a lifetime of hurt and anger against his father was validated. And as his father's long-time confidant declared his betrayal, William could no longer control the hostility that firmly gripped his heart.

He lunged forward and tore into Mikey, fighting him for the gun that now flailed above their heads. William's rangy body fell short against Mikey's beefy physique but he fought harder. Allowed his body to rid him of all the years of pent-up anger and hatred towards his father, yelled it out in Mikey's face, pushing and wrestling against the traitor.

Until a single gunshot exploded into the silence.

CHAPTER TWENTY-SIX

Still held captive by the tattooed man's gun, Adam, Kane, and Patrick watched as William's body went limp and slumped to the deck in front of them. A large pool of blood seeped from his abdomen and spread across the deck around him. From behind them, another gunshot sounded into the air—Walter's gun—when Sushruta forced his elbow into his face.

Walter fell back against an iron post, knocking his head.

Sushruta bolted, headed for the bridge.

Kane tore into Mikey.

Adam and Patrick simultaneously tackled the tattooed man.

Chaos ensued in a battle of good versus evil.

Kane pulled his gun.

Another shot went off—Kane's gun—narrowly missing Mikey's leg.

Mikey retaliated, slamming his forehead into Kane's and leaving him dizzy, struggling to stay in the present.

Mikey aimed his gun, but Kane's arm knocked it to the floor beside them as they engaged once more.

Behind them the tattooed man was outnumbered. Patrick threw a punch, Adam held him down. Another punch and the man's body slumped to the floor as he lost consciousness.

They turned to help Kane. Suddenly the boat thrust forward, its engines roaring as it pushed through the water.

Kane lost his balance, fell back onto Patrick and Adam and sent the crates breaking beneath their bodies.

Mikey bolted.

"I'll go after him, check on my father!" Kane shouted over his shoulder and chased across the deck after Mikey.

On the other end of the deck, Adam and Patrick found Walter seated on the floor.

"Walter, you okay?" Adam rushed to his side.

"Yeah, I'm fine. Go, help my son."

They decided that Adam would stay with Walter while Patrick went after Sushruta to try and stop the boat.

. . .

BELOW DECK, IN THE SHADOWY CORNERS OF THE vessel, Kane searched for Mikey. Gun stretched out in front of him, his body tense and ready to defend himself, he moved slowly. But Mikey was nowhere to be seen or heard. Jonesy's words echoed in his mind. *Don't be a hero, Kane. Call for backup.* He reached for his cell. No service.

His thumb scrolled to the messaging application and he sent a distress message to his partner anyway—it would send once the service came back. Somewhere behind him, there was movement. He ducked into one of the nearby cabins and listened, his back pinned to the wall. His fingers tightened on his gun. His mouth ran dry. Footsteps came towards him. He waited, pressed his shoulders further back against the wall. Once Mikey passed him, he'd attack from behind.

The footsteps grew louder. Sweat trickled down his temples. He didn't move. In the early dawn light that threatened to reveal his hiding place, his shadow stretched out beside him. He pinched his eyes, silently cursed it and hoped it wouldn't betray him.

The footsteps stopped. He sensed someone standing back to back with him on the other side of the wall. Neither of them moved, waiting for the other person to strike first. Kane's senses were at optimum. Then he heard the person's breathing, almost anxious, weak. Mikey wouldn't be afraid. He was far too arrogant for that. Or was he? He shuffled his weight, intentionally moving to expose his position, testing if the person had a gun.

When nothing happened, he moved away from the wall, his back to the small porthole, his gun stretched out toward the doorway, fully exposed. His index finger weighed on the trigger, pressed down, and stopped just before the first click. He was ready to defend himself, take him down.

"Give it up, Mikey!" he shouted.

He heard a big sigh, then movement. Patrick appeared in the doorway.

Kane's gun went off.

Patrick flinched.

Realization struck. Adrenaline shot through both men's veins.

Patrick cried out, slumped against the doorpost.

"Have you lost your mind?" Kane shouted and pulled him inside.

"Why did you shoot me?" Patrick responded.

"You're lucky it's just a graze, Phillips. I could've killed you. I thought I told you to stay upstairs."

Patrick sat on one of the bunks, clutching his arm where the bullet had grazed his shoulder.

Kane was already checking both directions of the narrow passageway with his gun.

"Where's Adam?" he asked.

"With Walter, upstairs on the deck. I left them to come help you. Didn't think you'd kill me."

"I didn't, you'll be fine, it's just a graze."

Kane peered into the corridor again. Still no sign of Mikey. Feeling outnumbered and in need of reinforcements, he checked his cellphone. Still no service. His mind worked on a solution.

"I need you to find a way off the boat. Take my father and Adam with you, get help. There has to be a life raft hidden somewhere. Think you can do that?"

Patrick nodded.

"I survived one storm, I'm sure I can do it again. What about Mikey and Sushruta?"

"We're on a boat so they're here somewhere. I'll go after them once I know you are safe and out of danger."

With a plan in mind, the two men went in search of a life raft. Remaining vigilant they moved toward the deck. Kane guessed Mikey was with Sushruta on the bridge.

Once on the deck, they moved toward the area where they had left Walter and Adam. They weren't there.

"I thought you said you left them here?" Kane said, his voice low, his body alert.

"I did," Patrick answered.

Kane's eyes skimmed the area. There was no blood anywhere, no sign of a struggle, only the open bird carriers.

At least the bird got away, he thought.

Behind them, something moved. Kane spun around, Patrick did the same.

They weren't prepared for what they saw.

Mikey's thick arm had Walter in a chokehold, his weapon firm against his temple. Beside him, the tattooed man had Adam in a similar position.

Kane's heart dropped to his feet, fear lodging in his throat.

"What's the matter, Detective Kane? Cat got your tongue?" Mikey mocked.

"Let them go, Mikey. There's no way you're stepping off this boat a free man."

Mikey bellowed a laugh so loud the waves around them were but a silent whisper.

"I don't think you are in any position to give me orders, Kane. You're outnumbered and outwitted. Now toss your gun over the side. Do it!" he yelled.

Reluctantly Kane did as he was told. His eyes locked with his father's and he saw the father he had always hoped he would have growing up. They were given another shot at their relationship, but he went and blew it.

Next to him, Adam looked calm, too calm. Like he knew something they didn't. Kane's eyebrows pulled into a curious frown as he tried to read him. But Adam's secrets were his own. He did know something they didn't. He knew his savior worked all things out for his glory. That he provides ample opportunity for man to turn from evil and choose salvation. That faith without works wasn't faith at all. That his work wasn't done.

"Now, move over there." Mikey instructed them to walk to the back of the boat.

Again Kane and Patrick did as they were forced.

Behind them he and his sidekick followed, dragging Walter and Adam along. When they reached the back of the ferryboat, he made them sit down, their backs against the hatch that would open the ramp.

Above their heads, Sushruta was on the bridge, glancing over his shoulder, steering the boat on a trip to nowhere. Lost in his own misery.

The sun's rays cast an orange glow across the ocean from behind the horizon, as if to remind them the creator of the universe was watching from above.

Mikey turned the gun on Adam.

"Hand it over."

He was talking about the ledger.

"I can't."

"You can and you will. Quit playing games, Adam."

Adam looked him square in the eyes.

"No, I mean, I literally can't. I don't have it."

Mikey's face turned grim, his eyebrows pulled together in anger. Anger because he had assumed it would be easy.

"Where is it?"

Adam had hoped it wouldn't come to this, but now the worst had happened. He needed to choose. If he gave up the ledger, Mikey would surely kill them on the spot, and there'd be no stopping his evil ways. But if he refrained from telling this man where he'd hid it, more peoples' lives would be at stake, and not only these people he now cared for. He thought of lying, protecting them, risking his life for theirs and the hundreds of innocent victims whose body parts they were selling. But where would that leave his faith, his trust in God? His belief that God had it all under control, that he didn't need to intervene. He couldn't lie, not even to save the lives of others. But he needed more time. Time to finish his work, time for God to do his.

"Take us back to the pier," his answer came.

Mikey's eyes narrowed as if to check that he wasn't being deceived. Then he smiled.

"Now that wasn't hard, was it?"

He called up to the bridge and told Sushruta to change course and head back to the pier.

As the day broke, Mikey had his sidekick tie his captives together. Bound separately at their hands and seated back to back with a rope snared around the group, they sat huddled together.

They were about an hour away from the shore, on a course set toward an outcome where all but one thought it would not end well.

CHAPTER TWENTY-SEVEN

Alone in the back of the boat, the small group waited until Mikey returned to the bridge and left his tattooed henchman to keep watch over them. He sat a fair distance away on an upturned crate, his head leaning back against a post, his body swaying with the motion of the vessel. The boat's engines roared beneath them, making it hard for him to hear his captives' conversation.

Out of earshot, Kane wasted no time.

"Anyone able to free their hands?" he asked.

"Not a chance, son, they've done a solid job," Walter said.

"Same here," Patrick and Adam agreed.

But Kane wasn't giving up. He wrestled with the rope behind his back, fueled by the anger that had welled up inside him.

"It's no use, son," Walter said when he noticed his son squirming next to him.

"There's always a way out," Kane said, his words grim and loaded with innuendo.

"I didn't have a choice, Harry," Walter replied, knowing he had directed the comment at him.

"There's always a choice. You just chose yourself instead," Kane said. His voice was heavy with years of hurt that had fueled his angry tone.

"It was never about me. It's the way your mother wanted it. Had I known then what I'd be getting myself into, I would've done things very differently, son. I've been trying to get your chief to listen to me for years now. He kept saying I was insane, and that there was no way Bill Sutton would be involved in this. I had no choice, this was the only way. I'm sorry it turned out the way it did. It's the last thing I wanted, believe me."

"I don't believe anything you say to me anymore, Pops! You've been lying to me for years. I didn't even know mom was sick! What a joke!"

"She didn't want you to know, Harry."

"So what, all those trips to Aunt Bee were a lie too?"

Walter didn't have to answer, Kane already knew the truth.

"Where did she go, Pops?" His voice was somber.

"Mostly the hospital, for her dialysis treatments. Other times, to spare you from seeing her in pain. She loved you more than anything in the world, Harry. It killed her to hide the truth, but she wanted you to remember her the way she was when she was healthy. She needed a kidney transplant and back then things weren't as advanced as they are now. The doctors didn't have any hope for her. Bill Sutton used us, knew we were vulnerable. He preyed on that. We didn't have the money for the transplant, and he was fully aware of that. I had to do something, or at least try."

"So you let him blackmail you all these years, even now, after he died. Why let it continue with William?"

Walter scoffed.

"William, now there's a piece of work. William didn't have a backbone to save his life. He couldn't stand up to his father, so he turned a blind eye. He was never included in any of his father's red market affairs. All he cared about was his trust fund, making sure the money never dried up. That's the only reason he was after the ledger, to destroy it, to save face. But Mikey? He was Bill's wingman, knew all the ins and outs. I wasn't the least bit surprised to hear he was the one who killed Bill. Money talks and friendship walks."

"I was blinded by them too," Patrick said. "All these years, it was right in front of my face. Heck, I managed all the money—blood money—and I didn't even know it. They were masters at keeping their clandestine operations hidden from the world. Who would've thought such evil lurked beneath their veils of benevolence?

Truth be told, if I were in your father's shoes I would've done the same. I'm sure your father did what he thought was right, Kane," Patrick added.

"I don't know what's right anymore," Kane spat, still wrestling with his tethered hands.

Adam, who had been quietly letting the conversation take its course, finally said, "Here's the thing about choices, you always have them. God gave us free will, but it's what we choose to do with that free will that counts. We all make choices, some good and some bad. Sometimes, they're choices we live to regret for the rest of our lives, but oftentimes they turn out to be opportunities to do things differently. The way I see it, this is one of those times. You're facing an opportunity. An opportunity to make a new choice. How you choose to part once we get off this boat is up to you, but make sure you can live with your decision."

Adam let his words linger as the ferry pushed through the water towards the pier. Kane's heart was heavy, burdened by years of unforgiveness and blame. But deep inside, he knew Adam was right. To his left, his father's head hung low on his chest, years of anguish visible in every etched line in his face. Their eyes met, their hearts softened, and with unspoken words the pain that had held them both in bondage for years slowly vanished.

"I'm sorry, Pops," Kane spoke gently. "I'm sorry I

didn't see it sooner, gave you the benefit of the doubt, rescued you."

"All's good that ends well, Harry. Things will be different from now on. All I ask is that you help me bring their entire operation down so no one else has to suffer. You are one of the finest detectives this country has ever seen, and once we get off this boat, you'll have everything you need to substantiate what you've seen here. Enough to put Mikey and Sushruta in prison for the rest of their lives." He gave a half-suppressed laugh. "Polly's been waiting for this day a very long time. Poor bird's been guarding it for years."

"I'd like nothing more than to bring this entire operation down, Pops, but first we need to figure out a way off this boat before they force Adam's hand into giving them that ledger. We're not that far from docking."

Kane wrestled with his ropes again, glancing over at their watchman who sat perched on his crate fast asleep.

"If ever there was a chance to overtake these guys, it'd be now. He's asleep." He pushed his chin forward to point out their keeper.

"These ropes are too tight," Patrick commented.

"Have a look around you, we need something sharp," Kane said.

"I've got long-nose pliers in my back pocket. I use them to fasten the pods on my birds," Walter said.

"Now you tell us!" Kane quipped. "Can you reach them?"

"Not unless you all move along with me so I can lift my behind off them."

"If it will get us out of this situation, I'm all in," Patrick said.

In the moments that followed the four men moved their bodies in unison to aid Walter in reaching the small pliers that were buried in his pants. The snared rope around their waists cut across their bodies while Walter forced his hands against the strain of the rope around his wrists. It took some effort and several attempts before he finally managed to grab hold of them between his two longest fingers.

"Got them!" he said, breathlessly, passing the pliers to Kane who started to work on the ropes right away.

In the distance, Adam spotted the skyscrapers over the rim of the boat.

"Hurry, we're almost there," he warned.

It was all the encouragement Kane needed and soon after, he managed to free one of his hands.

"I'm out," he said, elated. "Keep an eye on our tattooed friend over there."

He worked at Walter's knots, glancing over one shoulder every few seconds. Behind him, the city loomed closer. They were running out of time. Already focused on how to handle the situation once they reached the dock, he turned his attention to Adam.

"You said the ledger's at the pier. Where exactly have you hidden it? If you can steer Mikey away from it, I can handle this guy while Patrick and my father ambush Sushruta. That will buy us some time."

"That might be tricky," Adam replied.

"Why? You said it was hidden at the pier."

"It's not, and I never actually said I had hidden it at the pier. All I said to Mikey was that he should take us to the pier."

Kane's face spoke of his annoyance, while his mind worked hard on the problem that lay ahead.

"So, if it's not there, where is it?" Kane asked as he loosened the last strand around Walter's wrists.

But Adam's reply was interrupted when the tattooed man's deep voice roared at them from behind.

CHAPTER TWENTY-EIGHT

A s the sun's rays grew stronger over New York City, the small passenger ferry drew into Pier 63. Since the pier had been left abandoned many years before, it remained quiet and deserted. From the bridge, Mikey cast a wary eye out across the boardwalk. From somewhere below he heard a scuffle in the boat, stopped to listen, then heard his henchman's voice bellowing across the deck below. He peered over the railing and saw him fighting off Kane and Patrick while Walter worked to free Adam's hands. Reality set in when he saw his henchman fall back against the boat's railing, then flop in a heap onto the deck. He swore out loud, peered at the approaching shore, then pulled out his gun.

"Keep it steady, and lay back," he yelled at Sushruta where he stood behind him steering the boat.

He took aim, pointed the gun toward the group of

men, and fired off one bullet. It echoed in the morning air and slammed into one of the crates next to Kane.

"You going to shoot a cop now too, Mikey? That's life without parole, buddy," Kane yelled as he and the rest of them took cover.

"Only if they catch me, Kane, and I think I'll take my chances!" Mikey yelled back, moments before he fired again.

The bullet clanked against a piece of metal inches from where Kane was hiding. He ducked and ran to hide below the overhang of the bridge.

Kane's hand instructed the others to take cover, and he motioned he was heading around the bridge to ambush Mikey once he came down onto the deck.

Adrenaline had taken over his body. His mind was sharp, prepared for every eventuality. Except this time he was unarmed.

His eyes danced across the deck around him in search of a potential weapon. To one side lay a rusted wrench the size of his forearm. He leaped to pick it up, surprised that it was lighter than he had expected it to be. He gripped the handle, holding it firm against his thigh. A quick glance over his shoulder revealed his father, Patrick, and Adam running to take shelter just inside the door that led to the covered seating area.

Kane listened out for Mikey coming down the ladder steps above him. On the other side, William's undignified bloody corpse still lay, reminding him of the stakes. When there was still no sign of Mikey's descent, he moved forward, just enough to sneak a quick peek up the staircase.

But Mikey was nowhere to be seen. His eyes dashed in all directions, in search of his opponent.

Nothing.

Below deck, he heard banging noises.

His heart leaped. His stomach sank.

Mikey must have taken another way from the bridge to below deck. He turned and ran towards the door, expecting to see his team still waiting beyond it.

But they were nowhere to be found.

He hung back on the upper deck, just outside the door, his hand still firmly gripped around the rusted wrench. He inhaled, then counted to three, and yanked the door open, wrench stretched out in front of him.

The space was empty.

With his heart thumping in each temple, his eyes darting across the small, covered seating area, row by row, he searched. But all was calm around him. As he approached the steps that would take him below deck he hovered at the top, listening, body alert, heart beating out of control.

Noises echoed along the narrow corridor. He heard voices and realized they were in the death chamber. Unexpectedly, the boat stopped. His mind went to Sushruta. He glanced back, hearing his feet moving down the outside ladder stairs onto the deck.

Sushruta was coming from behind.

Kane peered around the corner, down the stairs, and into the space below. It was dark around him, with only the dimmest of light from a flashlight visible inside one of the plastic cubicles in the furthest corner. The thought that perhaps his father had led the other two men down to hide there crossed his mind. Perhaps it was Mikey who was somewhere behind him.

Trusting his instinct, he stealthily moved across the floor toward the dim light. Just outside the plastic curtain, he held back and listened. It was silent. The light suddenly faded.

He froze, waited.

He heard breathing. Then a shuffle. His body moved towards the opening. Vulnerable to the impending danger, he tried not to think about how it might end. Mikey would have a clear shot if he was on the other side of the plastic curtain. His finger slowly parted the opening in the sheet. It was too dark to see clearly, but he was certain he saw the outlines of his friends beneath the steel table. Deciding to trust his gut, he whisper-called. "Guys, you in there?"

The dim light went on, illuminating the area under the table, and revealing his father's face.

He rushed in towards them, not taking a moment to digest the strange expression in his father's eyes.

Until it was too late.

From somewhere behind he felt the blow to his

head, making him dizzy for a second. Then another blow came down onto his neck. This one made him fall to his knees. Kane turned to find the cause and saw the evil in Mikey's eyes, glowing in the dim light.

Staring down the barrel of Mikey's gun, Kane lay flat on his back.

Mikey didn't waste any time. His finger pushed down on the trigger as Kane rolled his body to one side, narrowly avoiding the bullet. He clambered to his feet, ran away from the table, and tried to disappear into the shadows. An orange flash of light lit up the dark space as Mikey fired off another shot. The bullet clanked against the steel next to him.

"Give it up, Kane! You're not getting out of here alive," Mikey declared.

Kane remained focused. Decided to fight back. He tossed the wrench like a boomerang, aiming to hit Mikey's chest. He missed. Mikey laughed.

"Nice try, Kane. Bet they taught you to throw like a girl in the academy."

Kane moved through the darkness, hiding between the cubicles, and drawing Mikey away from his team.

His father's voice echoed in the darkness Sushruta's voice followed. There was a grunt, then the dull sound of a fist colliding with someone's face. Bodies moved on the floor.

More groaning.

Heavy breathing.

Metal clanging.

Another shot.

Distracted by the commotion, Mikey turned to look back. Sushruta was on the floor, pinned down by the three men. Fear struck. He aimed his gun at the men, thought of shooting at them, but couldn't find a clear shot, and stopped himself. Instead, he pointed it back towards Kane.

But Kane was gone.

Mikey's eyes searched frantically, expecting Kane to pounce on him. He glanced back at the scuffle. Saw Sushruta dead on the floor.

A movement to his right had him turning towards it, but there was nothing.

The chamber's bright lights went on and lit up the entire space around him.

To his left, Kane suddenly came at him.

He aimed.

Pulled the trigger.

From the right, Walter's body cut in between them. The gun went off.

Kane charged into him, flattened his body to the floor.

In the distance, a female voice drifted towards them.

"NYPD, put down your weapon!"

Jones moved closer, her gun aimed at the man fighting with her partner. She yelled out to the man once more; he ignored her. She watched as Kane's hand pinned the gunman's wrist to the floor. The man's hand curled up, pointed his weapon at Kane's face. Jones fired, causing the man to drop his weapon in agony.

A SWAT team charged towards them, helped Kane to his feet, and arrested the gunman.

Kane turned to find his father. Walter lay on the floor, blood seeping from his right shoulder.

"Pops!" He rushed over and lifted him onto his lap. "Hang on, Pops, I got you. It's all over, hang in there. We need a medic!" he shouted out towards the SWAT team.

Panic flooded his insides as Walter's eyes glazed over.

"Don't you dare give up on us now, Pops! Don't you dare!"

"Polly... Polly," Walter repeated, his voice barely audible.

Kane felt himself being pushed aside, heard Jones telling him to move. Watched as a medical team worked to keep his father alive.

CHAPTER TWENTY-NINE

On the rooftop of the tall building on the wrong side of town, Detective Harry Kane watched as Adam retrieved the ledger from its hiding place. He had buried it beneath a pile of shavings just inside one corner of the pigeon coop.

"Really? It's been here the entire time. Not the most original hiding spot, but okay," Kane said amused.

"One doesn't always see what's staring you in the face," Adam smiled. "Besides, I was under attack and there weren't that many options available to me. I figured no one would come looking for it inside the loft."

Kane's fingers flipped through the pages.

"Thanks for your help on this, Adam. I don't know how you figured it out, but it's impressive."

"I had a little help from above, my friend. A lot of help, actually."

Kane fell silent.

"Well, if it weren't for you, I would've never reconciled with my father."

"It wasn't me, Kane. It was God who brought you together. I just followed his instruction and trusted him along the way."

"You really believe this was all God's doing?" Kane asked.

"Don't you?"

"I've never really thought about it much. I always thought God picked his favorites, and that I wasn't good enough. That people like Bill Sutton were the ones to go to heaven."

"Good deeds don't get you to heaven, Kane. It is by God's grace through faith alone."

"So you're saying Sutton's work meant nothing?"

"I'm sure his good work counted for something, mostly to those who benefitted from his charity, but to God, it's the inner work that counts. The one is no good without the other. When you allow God to work out the bad in your life, accept and trust him to refine you and prepare the inner good works, that's when you win his favor. All the wealth and good works in the world can't buy you salvation."

Kane shut the ledger and dropped it into an evidence bag.

"He's going to pull through, Kane. Walter's a fighter."

"That's what the doctors are saying too. In the meantime, I'd like to do him proud and find whatever evidence he said was here. This case needs to be rock solid to bring this entire operation down and lock Mikey away for good."

Kane entered the pigeon loft and reached out to where his father's beloved bird, Polly, sat perched on a branch.

"I can't believe this bird found her way back from the boat, all the way across the water."

"They are pretty smart, yes."

Kane held out his hand, inviting the bird to hop on. She did, then allowed Kane to detach a small device that was no bigger than his thumb from her harness just below her crop. It was a mini digital voice recorder. He pressed down on the small black button. The voices on the recording were unmistakable, taken on the boat when William had challenged Mikey and he'd confessed to killing Bill and the details of the entire operation.

"Well, how about that?" Adam said, awed. "Your father is one smart man."

Kane was equally impressed.

"My father was right. This confession is everything we need to tie this case down."

He added the digital recording to the evidence bag.

"You know, Adam, I did some digging of my own. Turns out this isn't your first case. You seem to have a knack for solving cryptic clues and breaking codes. You have a few friends in very high places. They told me they've been trying to get you to join them on a more permanent basis for some time now."

Adam smiled.

"You're a brilliant detective, Kane."

"So what's holding you back? You clearly have a unique gift. Why not work for them? This country could do with your help in taking down the rest of the bad guys out there."

Adam turned and stared out at the views over the city. The sun's rays glistened off the rooftops, illuminating the entire city. He tried to imagine the view God would have from heaven. It filled him with reverence, knowing his view paled compared to the Creator's. Kane's question was one that had burdened him for a while. He'd been praying for guidance since the first time Gabriel approached him, searched his heart, waited for God to reveal his will for his life.

But God hadn't answered.

There were days when he very nearly chose to accept the opportunity, reasoning that he fell short as a pastor and needed to put his gifting to better work. But there were equally as many times he just couldn't turn his back on The Lighthouse, his faith family, and pastoring in Turtle Cove. He had earnestly prayed, patiently waited for God to provide the answer.

Still it didn't come.

It wasn't until that very moment, perched high like the birds on top of Walter's roof, that the answer finally came to him.

And as was often the case when he shared a word of wisdom, the very substance of his recent teaching resonated within himself. God had given him free will too. The choice was his to make, not God's. The answer had been right in front of him all along. He realized everyone had gifts, and that those unique gifts led to different kinds of service, all offered to the same God. That all believers were co-workers, a universal team, working for one God. It didn't matter where he did his work; it was all done in the power of God's Spirit.

All that truly mattered was that he continued to walk in faith, studied the Word, and let God guide his path, so that it may equip him for every good work the Almighty chose to lay before him.

"All Scripture is God-breathed and is useful for teaching, rebuking, correcting and training in righteousness, so that the man of God may be thoroughly equipped for every good work."

2 Timothy 3:16-17

NIV

Download your FREE Character sheet

(https://urcelia.ck.page/bc56c3e024)

GET YOUR FREE SUSPENSE THRILLER!

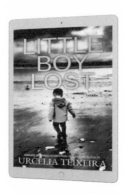

A MISSING BOY. A TOWN BURIED IN SECRETS. A DEPUTY WHO WON'T QUIT.

https://home.urcelia.com

VALLEY OF DEATH SUSPENSE THRILLERS

Ready to dive into the next series?

The Valley of Death series was inspired by Psalm 23

and promises to deliver a toe-curling suspense thriller trilogy you won't want to put down once you start!

Readers say this is my best work yet!

Best enjoyed in sequence

VENGEANCE IS MINE - Book 1

SHADOW OF FEAR - Book 2

WAGES OF SIN - Book 3

ALEX HUNT ADVENTURE THRILLERS

Fast-paced, clean archaeological adventure thrillers with a Christian worldview.

Inspired by actual historical events and artifacts

Also suited as standalone novels

The **PAPUA INCIDENT** - *Free when you sign up*

The **RHAPTA KEY**

The **GILDED TREASON**

The **ALPHA STRAIN**

The **DAUPHIN DECEPTION**

The **BARI BONES**

The **CAIAPHAS CODE**

For more on the author and her books, please visit www. urcelia.com

DEAR READER

All glory be to the Lord, my God who breathed every word through me onto these pages.

I have put my words in your mouth and
covered you with the shadow of My hand
Isaiah 51:16

It is my sincere prayer that you not only enjoyed the story, but drew courage, inspiration, and hope from it, just as I did while writing it. Thank you sincerely, for reading *Every Good Work*.

If you would like others to also be encouraged by this story, you can help them discover my book by leaving a review.
CLICK HERE

Writing without distractions is a never-ending challenge. With a house full of boys, there's never a dull moment (or a quiet one!)

So I close myself off and shut the world out by popping in my earphones.

Here's what I listened to while I wrote *Every Good Work*:

- 10 Hours/God's Heart Instrumental Worship —Soaking in His presence (https:// youtu.be/Yltj6VKX7kU)
- 2 Hours Non-Stop Worship Songs— Daughter of Zion (https:// youtu.be/DKwcFiNe7xw)

When I finished writing the last sentence of the book! How great is our God—Chris Tomlin (https://youtu.be/KBD18rsVJHk)

AUTHOR CONNECT

STAY CONNECTED

Sign Up for Urcelia Teixeira's newsletter and get future new release updates, cover reveals, and exclusive sneak peeks and VIP reader discounts! (signup. urcelia.com)

FOLLOW ME

BookBub has a New Release Alert. Not only can you check out the latest deals, but you can also get an email when I release my next book, and see what I read and recommend. Follow me here

https://www.bookbub.com/authors/urcelia-teixeira

Website:

https://www.urcelia.com

Facebook:

https://www.facebook.com/urceliabooks

Twitter:

https//www.twitter.com/UrceliaTeixeira

Urcelia Teixeira writes gripping Christian mystery, thriller and suspense novels that will have you on the edge of your seat! Firm in her Christian faith, all her books are free from profanity and unnecessary sexually suggestive scenes.

She made her writing debut in December 2017, kicking off her newly discovered author journey with her fast-paced archaeological adventure thriller novels that readers have described as 'Indiana Jones meets Lara Croft with a twist of Bourne.'

But, five novels in, and nearly eighteen months later, she had a spiritual awakening, and she wrote the sixth and final book in her Alex Hunt Adventure Thriller series. She now fondly refers to The Caiaphas Code as her redemption book, her statement of faith.

And although this series has reached multiple Amazon Bestseller lists, she took the bold step of following her true calling and switched to writing what naturally flows from her heart and soul: Christian Suspense.

A committed Christian for nearly twenty years, she now lives by the following mantra:

"I used to be just a writer. Now, I am a writer with a purpose!"

For more on her and her books, please browse her website, www.urcelia.com or email her on books@urcelia.com

Never miss a new release!
    Sign up to her Newsletter: signup.urcelia.com
    Follow her on BookBub (https://www.bookbub.com/authors/urcelia-teixeira)

    facebook.com/urceliabooks
    twitter.com/UrceliaTeixeira
    bookbub.com/authors/urcelia-teixeira